PLAYING DEAD

WITHDRAWN

It seemed darker than ever in the Old Rectory's spare room. Only by some reflected glow from the mirror on the dressing table and the full length mirror on the open wardrobe door, could one see the secondary glow of red stretched across the floor. The mirrors picked up the colour and held it because it wasn't moving. Nothing moved.

Three minutes later the murderer opened the bedroom door and crept silently into the room.

One second later there came the sound of a body tripping over something, and falling on to the floor with a heavy crash.

Thirty seconds later someone screamed and went on screaming.

Have you read?

POINT CRIME

PLAYING DEAD

Jill Bennett

SCHOLASTIC

Scholastic Children's Books
Commonwealth House, 1–19 New Oxford Street,
London WC1A 1NU, UK
a division of Scholastic Ltd
London ~ New York ~ Toronto ~ Sydney ~ Auckland
Mexico City ~ New Delhi ~ Hong Kong

First published in the UK by Scholastic Ltd, 1998

Copyright © Jill Bennett, 1998

ISBN 0 590 19176 4

Typeset by TW Typesetting, Midsomer Norton, Somerset
Printed by Cox & Wyman Ltd, Reading, Berks.

10 9 8 7 6 5 4 3 2 1

Prologue

CHANCE. When chance decides to take a hand, you haven't got a … chance!

Sleek and blood-red the Jaguar sped north, and aware of its power the driver happily relaxed. He felt at one with the beautiful piece of engineering that he owned. Beside him his wife drowsed, lulled by the smooth engine and the knowledge the car was safe in his hands.

The wasp in the pretty box on her lap drowsed too, drugged by the dark, and sugar from the contents of the box. Twenty soft, succulent, dreamy jelly babies lay side by side. When they were bored or tired with driving, the driver and his wife would pop a jelly baby into their mouths, and the melting sweetness always picked them up and they felt fresh again.

The driver was allergic to wasps. As a boy of ten he had been raced to hospital choking and suffocating from a wasp sting. They only just saved his life. He never forgot it.

Sleepily, his wife opened the lid of the box and pulled out a pink round jelly baby.

"Have one?" She carried it towards the driver's mouth and popped it in. Strawberry was his favourite.

The wasp, jolted out of its torpor, took to the air and still hazy, landed on the back of the driver's hand while he held the wheel.

He flapped his hand in panic, making the car swerve and the dozy wasp wake up and begin a circuit of the car. His wife, alerted now and terrified, opened a window.

The wasp took refuge somewhere on the driver's neck.

"Don't move!" his wife shouted.

But he couldn't help it. Panic gripped him. He flapped at it again.

In went the sting.

The pain in the driver's neck was nothing to the searing agony that gripped his chest. Paralyzed with pain, his staring eyes bulged and his limbs contorted. Only the central barrier stopped the careering Jaguar. In an almost empty road it hit, twisted and crumpled, and lay in a tangled heap of metal and steam on its back, silent at last.

The wasp, making its escape, found a new resting

place on a spilt black jelly baby and basked in the September sunshine.

Chance brought that man, that car and that wasp together — he didn't even know he was chancing his luck...

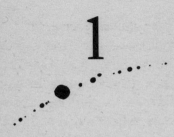

1

"Everything?" Gemma Davies stared at the solicitor, blue eyes wide with shock. "You mean, they left everything to me?"

Mr Pine of Pine and Redgold Solicitors nodded.

"The house, their money, and the family business and factory are now yours." He looked at her gravely. "The car," he added gently, "as you know, was a write–off."

Gemma shut her eyes briefly, against the vision of her parents' bodies in the tangled wreckage of their beautiful Jaguar.

"Nothing to anybody else at all?" she persisted, unable to believe what she was hearing.

"Nothing," Mr Pine replied simply.

He hesitated for a moment before going on

carefully, "I did hear some talk of a new will in preparation, Gemma, but," he spread his hands, "it was only in the planning stage."

Gemma sat where she was, pressing her hands together in her lap, trying to focus on what she had just heard.

"Only me?" she almost whispered.

Seeing her distress, Mr Pine sighed inwardly, walked round to the other side of his desk and leant his back against it. It wasn't easy for him either. He wanted to put his arm around her and tell her how much he also missed her mother and father – he had known them well and had watched Gemma growing up. But he knew he must keep the meeting as formal as he could, for Gemma's sake.

"Look," he said gently, "because everything is yours, or will be yours as soon as you are twenty-one, you are able to give anything you want to anyone, if you ever wish to do so.

"The other big subject is the matter of Davies Machinery Company, your factory. Yes, Gemma, your factory, and the fountain-head of all your money. I have been in contact with Mr Robins and we agree that everything can carry on as normal, for the moment anyway. Later, we can all sit round and review the way to go. So don't worry about that.

"Now," he said more briskly, "there will be a number of months before probate is over and all your parents' estate is settled. I am one of the executors of the estate, along with Mr Robins, so you can apply to me for anything you need until that is done. I have arranged for some money to be transferred to your existing bank account in the meantime. You are nearly eighteen and there will be just three years before you come in to your own. So, tell me if you have any problem at all – promise?"

Gemma nodded. She reached blindly for her suede bag and got to her feet.

"Thank you, Mr Pine," she said huskily.

"Hugh, that's what your parents called me."

His heart turned over as he saw her try to smile at him.

"Off you go, now," he told her briskly as if she was a little girl. He tried to ease the difficult moment. "And don't forget, anything you need..." He held the door open for her and Gemma, unable to say anything, passed through it.

Hugh Pine watched her small, slight figure, with its cap of shiny hair, walk down the stairs until she reached the landing and turned out of his sight.

She's so young, not eighteen yet, he thought, and so much richer than she has had time to realize. What will she do with her life?

Gemma walked to the bus-stop as if she was in her own tight little capsule and nothing else existed. She knew she must make herself understand her situation, but the capsule kept her safe as long as she could just keep hiding in it.

The solicitor's offices were in the busy commercial

centre of her home town of Standwick. This sprawling suburb had been eaten up by the much larger Midlands city. Her aunt and cousin lived on the outer rim of the suburb, just a few streets away from Gemma's own house. She had been staying with them since the accident that killed her parents.

As the bus took her along the familiar streets, she thought of Mr Pine. Gemma couldn't think of him as Hugh; his balding head, dark grey suits and large, imposing bulk seemed too formal for that. Of course, she had seen him many times at her house, and she noticed him at her parents' funeral. He was helping people find seats, and handing out service sheets. He looked a kind man, she thought, and she was glad he was there.

Trying to visualize the moment when she would have to tell her aunt Rita and her cousin Michael about the morning's meeting, her heart gave a lurch.

Rita had not been invited to attend, though she was the sister of Gemma's mother and her only close relative. Gemma now knew it was because she was the only person named in the will.

Delayed shock spread through her like a tidal wave as the bus drew up at her stop.

I feel sick, she thought desperately, as her capsule shattered around her. I'm going to be sick. Gemma stumbled from the bus into the cool September air. She took in a deep breath and leaned her head for a moment against a tree planted in the pavement.

Breathe slowly, she told herself. Slowly.

Little by little the waves of nausea drained away, leaving her knees feeling wobbly. She leaned against the tree a moment longer and closed her eyes.

"Gemma!" A voice close to her made her jump. She saw who it was and relief allowed her to smile.

"Mike," she said.

Her cousin was looking down at her anxiously. Most people looked down at Gemma but Michael had done so since he was twelve. He was very tall and thin, not a bit like his shorter, sturdy mother. His dark eyes under a fall of brown hair were worried.

"You OK? You've gone a funny colour, Gem."

"I'm fine," Gemma told him as steadily as she could, "but you're a welcome sight. Where've you come from?" She pulled her jacket a little tighter, burying her chin in the collar. Suddenly she felt cold.

"Nowhere special. Mum had to go to work, she's seeing someone late today, probably in a squat, so I was killing time."

Rita was a social worker for the council. Her work was mainly counselling and helping displaced or homeless young people. She often went to see people away from her office.

"You should have let me come with you," Michael said, still sounding worried. "Are you sure you're not going to faint or something?" He couldn't forget her still, white face the day of the funeral, when she had collapsed and he helped to carry her to the waiting car.

"I'm fine, really," she told him firmly. "I could use

a hot drink, though."

Linking arms, they walked along the tree-lined road that led to his house. It was a semi-detached at the end of a row of similar houses. A wooden gate with a clearly printed sign on it stated the house was called Bay Trees. It opened on to a neat front garden, bright with dahlias. Michael used his key in the front door and the welcome warmth of the hall greeted them.

Rita's house reflected her personality. Her home was cheerful and clean and very neat. Some of Michael's friends thought she over-did the tidiness to the point of obsession. It had none of the gracious opulence of the Old Rectory, where they felt more relaxed.

Rita and her younger sister, Beryl, were small women and both had fair, delicate colouring, but the likeness ended there. While Rita was bustling and practical, her figure thickening as she got older, Beryl had remained almost unchanged from the rather dreamy girl she had been in her youth.

Rita had married first. She had fallen for a trainee hospital technician. At last, after about eight years of trying, Michael was born. When he was eleven his father left them to marry someone else. Rita was devastated. He moved away from Standwick and started another family, leaving her to keep them both. Michael rarely saw his father now.

Beryl, the younger, had not married right away. She had begun to write her romantic novels and was content. But, in time, she was swept off her feet by the energetic son of a local factory owner. The factory produced machines for the production of pharmaceuticals and was very lucrative. Mark Davies went on to make his father's business an even bigger success.

Very soon after their marriage, Gemma arrived, and the two cousins, close in age, grew up together. Mark and Beryl Davies were a great support to Rita when her husband left and a nervous breakdown overtook her. Michael lived at the Old Rectory for a while until his mother got back on her feet. It was with their help she was able to buy Bay Trees.

Gemma began to feel a little better and her head was not aching as she had feared it would. She always carried painkillers in her bag these days.

She still dreaded telling Michael the content of the will. Telling him, in effect, that his uncle and aunt, so loving and kind, had not made provision for him. Or if they had, and the new will would have included him and Rita, that it was all too late.

If he was disappointed, Michael didn't show it.

"Poor little rich girl!" he said with affection and came up and gave her a tight hug.

Gemma's relief made her feel lightheaded. What had I expected Mike to do, she thought – never talk to me again, or something? But Rita…?

"Mike," she said, "would you mind telling Rita? It's just that it would be better if I didn't…"

"Sure, I'll tell Mum. She'll be glad for you, you know."

"Think so? Won't she feel, well, left out? I feel bad about it all."

Michael smiled at her.

"Mum's a great realist; what will be, will be. She loves you, her only hope will be that you will still love her."

Tears gushed into Gemma's blue eyes and flooded her cheeks.

"Of course I'll love her, always … and you, Mike…" This time she flung her arms around his neck and buried her face in his jumper. Her voice rose out of it, muffled. "You're all I've got now."

Mike took a deep breath and held her tightly. He had loved his aunt and uncle, the two families had been very close. He too was adrift with grief. They would just have to support each other – only three of them left.

Gemma untangled herself from his jumper which hung about his spare frame in folds, and turned to put on the kettle.

Michael turned away and sighed deeply. In spite of what he said to Gemma, he was struggling with an acute feeling of rejection about his lack of inheritance. But whatever happened, he knew he must never show what he felt to Gemma, ever.

2

The first few nights after her parents' deaths and her removal to Bay Trees had been appallingly difficult for Gemma. She had tried everything to get to sleep. She watched late-night TV, took endless night-time drinks and read until her eyes were raw, but sleep evaded her. The doctor gave her some mild tranquillizers which helped, but she had no intention of becoming hooked on them.

Her father's heart was the only bit of him that was not as strong as an ox. The post-mortem showed he'd suffered a massive heart attack. There was no mention of the wasp. Loving speed, as Gemma knew he did, it caught him unprepared even though he was given a warning attack two years before. Her mother died instantly with him; no one could have escaped that accident.

Gemma clung to the moment when her mum and dad said goodbye to her. Rita and Michael were there, too, and they were all light-hearted and happy, seeing them both off to Glasgow for a huge trade fair. There was to be a grand ball, and they would meet many of their old friends.

She never saw them again.

Rita had formally identified their bodies, but now Gemma wished she had gone with her. Then she could hold the real image of them in her mind and not the imagined horror of their battered, mangled faces. Rita told her they were at peace and their expressions tranquil. Gemma tried to remember that.

Now the funeral was over, Gemma was gripped at last with an over-riding weariness. She went to bed earlier and earlier each night and fell asleep at once.

It was a great relief to her that Rita would come home after she had retired to bed. Then Michael could tell his mother about the will. She knew she would have to face her in the morning, but the worst would be over and Rita would know.

So at eight forty-five she left Michael watching TV and by nine o'clock she was asleep.

But not for long.

Crash!

Gemma sat bolt upright in bed, every nerve alert. She was dreaming that she was sitting on a bus which was careering down a steep hill, out of control. The people in the bus were reading papers and chatting as if nothing was wrong. Gemma was desperately trying to tell them to jump off before it was too late. They were going to crash.

The bus came off the road with a terrifying screech of brakes. She heard herself shouting over the sound of splintering glass and impacting metal.

The noise jerked Gemma into a sitting position. It sounded loud, it sounded as if it was in the house, and worse than anything, it was like the imagined crash she heard over and over in her mind when she thought about her parents.

Listening hard, she tried to hear the sounds of the house over her loud heartbeats. Nothing. With her ears straining, she put her legs over the side of the bed and padded to the door and opened it. The hall light was on, so were the lights in the kitchen and drawing-room. She could hear the low murmur of the TV. It sounded like the news. Whether it was news at nine or ten, she didn't know. It wasn't important. Mike and Rita were in the kitchen, that was clear from their familiar voices.

Gemma felt reassured. It was just a dream – another nightmare like all the ones before. Would she ever be free of them? she wondered miserably.

Returning to bed she lay with her eyes closed, trying to doze off again, when a thought suddenly came to her. It was like someone had said it out loud, clearly and distinctly.

Go home, Gemma. It's time to go home.

Gemma savoured the thought warily. There had been moments when she wondered if she could ever go home again and face the empty rooms. Home. Gemma found she was actually smiling at the idea. Home. A feeling of warmth and comfort crept over her as she thought of it. Yes, she would do that, that's where she should be; she'd tell Rita in the morning.

Turning over drowsily, Gemma fell asleep.

Breakfast, however, wasn't easy. Rita was pale and looked tired. Gemma's heart sank. She knew that Rita's schedule of work was very demanding; it couldn't be easy visiting people with problems in all sorts of places after hours. She desperately hoped that the business of the will had not upset her further. If only she was able to talk about it, but she didn't know how to bring the subject up. So she took another bull by the horns.

"Rita," she said carefully, "I was thinking that I should be going home soon."

"No hurry," Rita said absently.

"Um … I thought I'd go sometime this week…"

Michael looked up from his bowl of cereal and Rita stared across the table at her in surprise.

"But Gemma, dear, you'll be all on your own, have you thought of that? Have you thought of how it will be at night in that large house?"

Gemma, trying hard to behave naturally, poured milk over her cereal but she couldn't meet Rita's eyes. The weight of her inheritance bore down on her, and she glanced wildly around the room.

"I have to go," she blurted out and immediately regretted the way it sounded.

Rita drew in her breath and Gemma knew she had hurt her.

Everything I say is wrong this morning, she thought miserably. Remembering Hugh Pine, she had been hoping to tell Rita that her mother would want her to have something to remember her by, anything she liked, and Michael, too. This obviously wasn't the time to bring it up.

Rita let out her breath and reached automatically for the milk.

"Don't leave us, Gemma dear, not yet. You're still very shocked and you'll have more nightmares all alone. Stay a little longer, don't leave us so soon."

Gemma's face composed itself into an anxious mask. She didn't want to hurt her aunt further, but she just knew it was time to go home. Time to begin her new life, to find out who she was now that so much had changed.

"I'll ask Becca to stay with me, I'm sure she will."

Rita looked at her niece's set face and saw, in her eyes, the mirror image of her dead sister's expression when she had firmly made up her mind about something. She sighed and gave in.

Two days later, on Wednesday afternoon, Rita re-arranged her appointments and reluctantly helped Gemma pack, then took her home.

"You're not to worry, Rita. I'm fine now, honestly."

Gemma hoped her voice sounded convincing. They were standing inside the front door of the Old

Rectory and her hand was on the latch, waiting to open it for her aunt to leave.

"I really don't like leaving you here, Gemma. Are you sure about it? Our house is always yours, you know that."

"Rita, I need to be here. It's my home. You and Michael aren't far away, I can always call you, can't I?"

"Any time, of course. But I hate to think of you here alone."

Gemma opened the door as she said, "I won't be alone, remember? Becca will be here later. She's coming to stay for ages."

Sighing heavily, Rita stepped out into the early autumn sunshine.

"If you were miserable here, Gemma, Beryl would never forgive me. You're my only sister's only child, you know."

At the sound of her mother's name Gemma's throat constricted. She was coping so well up to then. Just go, Rita, she willed.

To her relief, Rita turned and kissed her, gave her a long hug and hurried down the path and out through the wooden gate on to the road. She shut the gate behind her and lifted her arm in a small wave before walking briskly away.

Gemma watched her aunt's sturdy figure disappear behind an overgrown laurel hedge that ran along the edge of the front garden. She hoped she hadn't been unkind, wanting to be home so much.

Rita's house had been a wonderful refuge but now she needed to be where she belonged.

At first, she had imagined that she would never be able to cross the threshold of her home again, knowing her mother's loved voice would not be waiting to greet her as she came in, to call her name and ask her about her day. Her mother, being a writer, always worked at home. But now Gemma knew she wanted to be there and nowhere else.

She yearned, with a passion that surprised her, to touch familiar things. The knives and forks, the colourful mugs, even the electric kettle that was forever cutting out before it boiled. The feel of the carpet on the landing under her bare feet, and the view from her bedroom window – all were calling her and seemed to promise comfort.

Gemma stood in the doorway of the house and let her eyes wander over the front garden. It was large for a town, but then so was the house. Large, rambling and comfortable, just what an old rectory should be. It had been built when Queen Victoria was a young mother, to house a vicar's roisterous family. It had been lived in by many other sorts of families after the church sold it. Then Gemma's parents fell in love with it.

She noted that a few weeds were struggling up through the gravel path, and there were many dead roses on the white standard trees that stood on either side of it. Untended, the September blooms had dropped their petals on to the uncut grass, like tears, she thought.

Without warning, Gemma saw her mother's figure in front of her on the path. Small and slender, she was halfway down, cutting off the dead roses and placing their ruined heads into a basket. The picture was so vivid that she could not believe she was only seeing it in her mind. She saw her mother's actions clearly. They were deliberate and unhurried, like everything she did. She clipped the stalks with her secateurs and laid the fallen heads into her basket as if they were still worth preserving.

Gemma turned sharply away, pushing the front door shut behind her. She could not be confronted with images like that, so clear and fresh, not if she was to stay there. Panting a little, she leaned on the newel post at the foot of the stairs in the spacious hall and stared at her suitcase waiting on the carpet. For a moment she wondered what it was doing there.

Mrs Jenkins, who came to clean for the family twice a week, was obviously still doing her job. Mr Pine had seen to that. There was no air of neglect anywhere inside. In fact, there was a bowl of late roses on the table in the hall. There was another little posy waiting for her on her dressing table when she lugged her case upstairs. Gemma felt a rush of gratitude for Mrs Jenkins, who had looked after the Old Rectory since she was very little.

She put her suitcase on her bed but didn't open it. I'll unpack later, she thought, when Becca comes. Now, I'll just savour being home and, for the moment, alone.

*   *   *

At that precise moment Gemma was not alone. Someone moved stealthily down the hall to the back door and slipped outside, locking the door behind them without a sound.

Gemma moved over to the window and looked out at the familiar view.

"It's still the same," she whispered to herself, wondering how that could be when her world had been so completely shattered.

The Old Rectory's garden spread its late-summer self down to the apple and plum trees, now laden with fruit, to the point where the ordered beds gave way to longer grass. Over the garden's high wall the church tower of St Mary's rose, its stone as grey and permanent as ever. It was hard to tell from here that St Mary's had ceased to be a church about the same time the last vicar left the Rectory, some twenty-five years ago. No services had been held in it since and most of the main windows were boarded up.

An old wooden door in the wall still stood in its place, leading from the Rectory garden into the churchyard. Its bolt was rusted badly and grass and ivy had all but smothered it. No one had passed through it for years.

From her vantage point Gemma could see two small, pointed, unboarded windows in the tower, and if she leaned far out, a corner of the graveyard. This was empty of its tombstones, for they had been removed to stand like uninvited guests around the edge of St Nicholas's churchyard two streets away. St Nicholas's was a comparatively new church, built complete with church hall and meeting house, so when a choice had had to be made between them, St Mary's hadn't stood a chance. Now it stood empty and unwanted.

Standing at the window, with her vision going slowly out of focus, Gemma sank into a state of suspended thought. For a few quiet minutes her heart and mind floated free, not thinking, not feeling, in something deeper than a brown study. It was peaceful and part of her wanted to stay like that for ever.

Suddenly she snapped back into focus. Had she seen movement in the far-off patch of churchyard? She leaned forward as far as she could and stared hard. There was no movement there now.

Imagination, Gemma thought. She had seen people, children mainly, playing there before. She did so herself, years ago. It made a daring, mysterious playground.

The front door bell gave a long, loud ring and she came to herself with a start. Still tingling a little from the jolt of the bell, she belted down the stairs and flung the door open.

3

"Becca!"
"The same."

"Oh, Becca!" Gemma threw her arms around the large, familiar untidy figure standing on the threshold.

Rebecca's long arms enfolded her friend, making Gemma's small form nearly disappear in the fold of jacket and scarves that were slung, rather than worn around her neck.

The two girls unwound.

"Bring your things inside," Gemma said, brushing away the tears that came so easily these days for grief or gladness. "I'm so glad your parents let you come."

Rebecca's huge bag fell from her shoulder with a clonk as she leaned forward to pick up her battered old carpet-bag. She wrenched it back as she tried to pick up two of the assorted supermarket plastic bags that lay, with at least three others, round her legs.

"Travelling light, I see." Gemma found herself grinning at her friend. She picked up the bags Rebecca couldn't manage. "In you go," she said, "I'll bring the rest."

They both unpacked, then the two girls sat at the large oval table in the kitchen. It was evening now, and they had just finished eating a meal of pie and oven chips from the freezer. Gemma was scooping out ice-cream from a carton into two bowls.

The evening was blustery and rather cool. It was good to be in the well-appointed Old Rectory kitchen, the heart of the house, and a cosy place.

No two girls could possibly have been more different. While Gemma was slight and five feet three, Rebecca was heading for six feet tall. Like her mother, Gemma's bones were fine drawn. Her fingers tapered delicately and her narrow feet seemed to skim the ground rather than tread on it. Rebecca, when her friends were being polite, was described as rangy. Her arms were long, her shoulders wide, and her legs sometimes seemed to be quite out of her control.

Gemma's fair, straight hair fell in a smooth cap around her ears. The wind might blow or the tempest roar but it always resumed its perfect shape immediately afterwards. Rebecca, on the other hand, experimented with her russet locks. They were naturally very curly and, if left to themselves, fell about her shoulders in a bouncy cloud. But they were seldom left to do that. Rebecca wound ribbons, scarves, flowers into them. She tied them up this way and that, depending on her mood. At present they were fairly subdued. A multi-coloured Indian scarf bound them loosely and was left free to trail down her back.

Rebecca's moods were violently felt. They took her over. As a loyal friend she was hard to beat. In contrast, Gemma moved gently through her days. Her nature was an even one and, although she felt things every bit as deeply as Rebecca, she preferred to sort out her problems alone, or talk about them quietly to people she could trust.

Perhaps it was just this quality of Gemma's that drew Rebecca to her. Perhaps she could see in Gemma's calm the safe harbour for her own tempest. Perhaps Gemma was drawn to Rebecca's zest for life and action, preferring to be the onlooker rather than the doer. Anyway, they had been close friends all their senior school days, and their relationship became stronger as they entered their late teens.

"How's Sam enjoying work?" Gemma asked. Rebecca's brother, Sam, had just begun stacking shelves at the local supermarket. It was the start of his work-experience year.

Rebecca pulled a face. Sam declared he wanted to rise to the top in the commercial world of buying and selling. Stacking the shelves in a supermarket was certainly beginning at the bottom.

"He's being paid for it, so it's a start, I suppose."

Gemma wondered how Sam could bear to be confined in a supermarket all day. He was such a high spirited, happy-go-lucky sort of person. She liked him very much, and lately, just before the end of the summer holidays, there had been a deepening of their friendship, something Gemma stored away and cherished. All their school life they hung about in a foursome. Gemma and Michael, Rebecca and Sam. It was funny to think of him in the world of work now and she missed him.

Changing the subject, she said, "Michael said he'd come round later."

"Great." Rebecca reached for her bowl. "I saw him yesterday for the first time since the…" She stopped. She nearly said "since the funeral".

It's a bit like treading on a tightrope, she thought sadly. So many ways to tip Gemma off balance, we have to be very careful. I hope the others realize.

Gemma noticed her hesitation and, with her swift intuition, understood.

"Look, Becca," she said, a firm edge coming into her voice to keep it steady, "you don't have to go about on tiptoe with me, you know. It's better if you just say what you want to say. I know you wouldn't try to hurt me. We mustn't act like strangers, I don't need that."

"OK, sorry. But you know, Gem, it's so hard to do anything to make it any better…" Rebecca stretched out her hand and placed it over Gemma's, giving it a squeeze. It was the one with the spoon in it and her action dislodged the lump of ice-cream about to leave it, not into the bowl, but on the table.

Rebecca groaned and rose to get a cloth to wipe it up. Gemma laughed. It was so typical of her friend. She would impulsively do a kind action only to find that she dropped a priceless crystal glass in the process.

"Look," she said, "you're here with me, aren't you? I wouldn't want anyone else, so don't be so thick, right? Coffee for you, Becca? I'll have my chocolate, or would you like some too?"

"Chocolate! I'll munch it with the best – but drink it – yuck! I don't know how you can."

Gemma grinned at her and finding relief in the simple action, she got up and put on the kettle.

The door bell rang.

"Michael," Gemma said and went to open it.

Rebecca finished her ice-cream, put her spoon down with a clatter and sighed. She was glad to be there, was very touched when Gemma asked her, but she felt the next few days until the routine of school life began again the following week were going to be tricky. She hoped she could cope.

Gemma returned with Michael behind her.

"Hi," he said to Rebecca.

"Greetings," she returned. "Coffee?"

"Yeah." Michael watched Gemma setting out the mugs and spooning in the coffee grains in silence. She took down her chocolate tin as she always did. It was all so familiar, but he felt awkward now. Uneasy with his cousin, restless, he prowled about, staring at well–known objects, not knowing what to say.

Rebecca watched him. Why does grief turn the people we know into strangers? Why is it so hard to be normal? she wondered.

"Oh, do sit," Gemma told him, beginning to catch his mood. She was holding down the switch on the kettle to make sure it boiled. "It will have to go," she muttered as she turned to the fridge for the milk.

"Um, good holiday, Bec?" Michael was making small talk.

Then Gemma screamed.

4

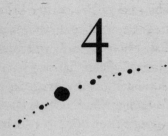

The sound split the room. Rebecca's chair legs screeched on the tiles as she started, and Michael froze.

Gemma slammed the fridge door so hard it shook and a bowl of fruit standing on the top fell off and crashed to the floor. Apples rolled everywhere and the earthenware bowl broke into pieces.

Michael looked in horror at his cousin's white face. She rushed to the sink and clutched the edge of it convulsively. She felt deathly sick.

Rebecca went to her. "What is it, Gem? For God's sake, tell us!"

Gemma battled to master her heaving stomach and taking a few gulps of air, she said as calmly as she could, "There's a rat in there."

"Rat?"

"Dead." Gemma spoke in spurts. "Head's bashed in."

"How d'you know?" Shock made Rebecca stupid.

Gemma shut her eyes, taking in a long deep breath.

"Obvious," she said as she let her breath out in a slow sigh, trying to shut out the image of the creature's matted, crushed skull and the blood that had smeared the clean glass shelf.

"My God." Michael was the first to move. He put a hand on the fridge handle and kept it there for just a beat before he opened the door in a rush and looked inside.

He was quick to shut it again, but Rebecca had seen the revolting body and felt herself growing faint. The sight of blood nearly always affected her like that. If she even pricked her finger and the blood beaded, she had to get rid of it fast and sit down for a moment.

"I'll ditch it, Gem. Best not to think about it. You girls go away." Michael steeled himself.

Rebecca looked helplessly at Gemma. She was fighting the familiar swimming sensation and the edges of her vision were threatening to go dark. She gripped the back of a kitchen chair for dear life.

Gemma longed to do just what Michael told them and run out into the garden – anywhere. But forcing her voice not to tremble, she said, "There's some newspapers in the broom cupboard, Mike. I'll get a plastic bag."

Between them, and as quickly as they could, they managed to wrap the rat's stiff body in paper and envelop it in a strong plastic bag, both trying not to look at it. They picked up the pieces of the broken bowl and put them in another bag, salvaging the apples. Michael took it all to the dustbin outside. He flung the bundles in, slamming on the lid with relief. By the time he returned, Gemma had taken out the few items that had been in the fridge and was washing them with hot water and disinfectant. Her pale face was still tinged with green, but her mouth was set in a straight, compressed line. Rebecca was sitting at the kitchen table and colour was slowly returning to her face.

The horrible job had been done in silence. When it was over, with one accord, they took their mugs and left the kitchen. No one wanted to talk about what had just happened; at least, not in there. It seemed like an episode from a piece of fiction, not real life, and they felt stunned. No one could even begin to contemplate how, and indeed why, a dead and mangled rat had appeared where it had. At the back of everyone's mind was the thought someone must have put the creature in the fridge. It couldn't have just materialized; someone had done it to shock Gemma.

When they were all outside in the passage Gemma pulled the kitchen door firmly shut, as if to prevent what had happened in there from infecting the rest of the house. She didn't lead them into the sitting-room. That room still had to be faced without her parents' familiar presence in it and she wanted to do it when she was alone. So she took them upstairs to her bedroom, the room she always thought of as her sanctuary, somewhere familiar, somewhere safe.

"How did that ghastly thing get in the fridge?" It was the question they all wanted to ask but Michael got there first.

Rebecca flung herself down on Gemma's divan bed.

"Maybe Mrs Jenkins has flipped at last." It was a hopeless attempt to make them smile. It didn't succeed.

Gemma was thinking hard. Mrs Jenkins, regular as the talking clock, came in at ten and left at one. She and Rita had come to the Rectory at about two, after lunch. Mrs Jenkins was asked to get in bread and milk, so she would have put them in the fridge, and Rita had brought some eggs with her, the apples that had been in the fated bowl and a packet of bacon. That, too, went into the fridge and there certainly wasn't anything resembling a dead rat then.

"It wasn't there when I came home," Gemma said slowly. "I would have seen it, or Rita would." She wondered how long she had been in her bedroom staring out of the window. It hadn't seemed very long. Was it long enough for someone to come in without her knowing?

"What time did you turn up, Becca?"

"Three-ish." Rebecca was vague. Time was not one of her strong points.

Gemma wrapped her arms around herself and shivered. After Rita left she had only been in her bedroom. That was down the first-floor passage and out of earshot of the bulk of the house. She hadn't noticed the time, hadn't heard a sound, hadn't seen a thing.

Michael, who knew the routine of the house and the probability that his careful mother had brought supplies for Gemma, made the same conclusion.

"Should we tell the police?" Gemma asked. "It could be a break-in."

She was trying not to hear Rita's voice in her head warning her about being afraid. She hadn't reckoned on dead rats then. She realized she was still shivering.

"What could we say?" Rebecca raised her shoulders in a shrug. "Sorry to trouble you, Sarge, but there's a dead rat in my fridge?"

"Look, Gem." Mike felt he had to get Gemma back to Bay Trees where he could keep an eye on her. "You really don't have to stay here. Come home again with me."

"No." Gemma spoke too loudly and Rebecca started. "I won't leave here, Mike. I can't go backwards and that's how it would seem, at least to me. I have to go forward, and forward means being here."

She turned to Rebecca. "Bec, do you mind staying with me after this?"

In spite of her involuntary feeling of unease, Rebecca said staunchly, "Rock of Gibraltar, me. Unbudgeable." She folded her arms and tried to look permanent.

Gemma's blue eyes spoke their thanks to her and she turned back to her cousin.

"Don't you dare tell Rita about this. She'll have fifty fits and I won't get a moment's peace."

Michael sighed. What could he do if she wouldn't be looked after? He was standing in the middle of Gemma's bedroom, his tall figure stooping slightly.

"Your choice, Gem," he said. "I think you're wrong, but it's your decision. Anyway, you'll probably be selling the place as soon as things get sorted out."

Gemma's eyes blazed.

"Who says?"

Rebecca, surprised, saw her quiet friend was rigid with anger.

"Won't you? You'll be really crazy if you don't. It's far too big for you."

Michael's voice was reasonable. For a second he had had a wonderful vision of the three of them living together: Rita, Gemma and himself. In a big roomy place somewhere, with all old memories forgotten. Selling the Old Rectory seemed the first logical step.

"Selling my home is the last thing I'll do!"

Michael stared at her, taken aback by the strength of her reaction.

But Gemma wasn't ready to cope with the grief that suddenly threatened to engulf her. Haven't I lost enough? she cried silently. Here, I still have something. Mum and Dad don't seem so far away. She turned towards the window to try to retain control of herself. Rebecca saw and got up to go to her. She hissed at Michael, "You prat, look what you've done!"

He was full of remorse. All he wanted to do was protect her.

"I'm so sorry, Gem." He rose. "I'd better go before I really mess things up."

Without looking at him, Gemma nodded. She was still wrestling with her feelings, unable to help him feel better.

"I'll ring you in the morning." Michael went to the door and turned to his cousin as if about to say something more. He desperately wanted to tell her that he cared about her, would never want to hurt her, but instead he just said, "Bye, Gem."

Rebecca followed him out and down to the front door, knowing Gemma had to have a moment on her own.

"They were great, you know, Beryl and Mark," Michael said to her as he stood on the threshold. "I just have this strong feeling that I have to keep an eye on Gem for their sakes, know what I mean?"

Rebecca nodded. She did know. Michael had been keeping an eye on Gem in his way since they were just kids. He was her champion and big brother rolled into one. She felt desperately sorry for him, too. She knew about his father walking out on them when he was still at primary school and Gemma's family being like his own. His loss was great as well.

"Do you think," Michael went on, "that rat business is just a nasty, sick joke?"

Rebecca snorted.

"Some joke!" But she caught a new note of anxiety in his tone.

"Could someone be trying to … scare her away?"

"Scare her away?" Rebecca echoed him. "You mean, get her out of the house by frightening her?"

"Well, it's possible. That would be some sort of a motive. But who…?" Michael gave an abrupt sigh and stepped on to the path.

"Keep your eyes skinned, both of you," he said, a little ominously, over his shoulder as he waved goodbye.

And on that happy note, thought Rebecca uneasily, as she watched him go.

5

Six weeks passed and Rebecca was still living with Gemma. Her mother and father approved of the arrangement. The Peels lived close by and felt their daughter was perfectly capable of coping away from home. They were both doctors. Rebecca's mother was a partner in a local general practice and her father worked as a consultant at a hospital in the centre of the city. Their busy lives meant Sam and Rebecca got used to fending for themselves. It was no longer just a visit. Rebecca had moved in and it was working out very well.

October was on the way out and the girls were walking home after afternoon classes were over. The autumn light faded earlier now the clocks were altered. The end of summer time, Gemma thought, a formal announcement that summer was now over.

She rubbed her nose, which was getting cold. A frisky wind was blowing the dying leaves as they drifted from the branches of trees overhanging the pavement. It lifted them again and made them eddy about the girls' ankles as they strode briskly along.

"Guy Fawkes' Day next Saturday," Gemma said. She always loved the tradition of bonfires and fireworks and hot smoking sausages.

Rebecca looked sideways at her. "Not only Guy's Day, is it?"

Gemma said nothing. It was also her eighteenth birthday. Guy Fawkes and Gemma always celebrated November the fifth together.

Rebecca tried to peer round at her friend's face to gauge her mood. Gemma's parents regularly threw huge parties for Gemma and Mr Fawkes. This, her eighteenth, would surely have been memorable. She wondered what Gemma was feeling, what she would like to happen now.

They were passing the wall of the deserted churchyard. It was a waist-high stone wall capped with rusting iron railings.

"Hey!" Rebecca stopped walking, putting an arm out to Gemma.

"What?" Both girls stared at the church.

"It's gone. I could have sworn I saw a light inside."

"It's this twilight, it plays tricks," said Gemma. The street lights had just come on. "I thought I saw something in the churchyard from my window, but it was nothing. Easily done."

"Silly me," Rebecca shrugged. "Still," she went on as they began to walk again, "I've often imagined there's something going on behind those boarded windows." She gave a mock shiver.

Michael caught up with them as they turned the corner of the street leading to the Old Rectory. As they paused to open the gate someone else loomed out at them from behind a shrub in the garden.

"Sam!" cried Rebecca, startled.

"Bean-brain!" said Gemma more mildly, but her heart glowed. To the others the quality of their friendship had not seemed altered, but she knew Sam managed to single her out in a special way more and more. She hoped he realized she knew and that it made her very happy.

Michael looked at him severely. "Layabout! What are you doing away from work?"

"Oh," Sam replied with a casual air, "they gave me a couple of hours off."

"More like you took them. Do be careful, Sam." Rebecca poked him in the ribs and he retaliated.

"Now you're here," Gemma broke into the slight scuffle that had started, "you'd better stay for tea."

Sam pretended to jostle them through the front door.

"I thought you'd never ask! Ow! I surrender!" This because the girls were thumping him with their school bags, heavy with books.

Gemma and Rebecca dashed upstairs to change

from sober school gear into jeans and loose, vivid shirts.

While they were gone Sam touched Michael on the shoulder.

"Mike", he said rather hurriedly, "I haven't seen you this week, and I've been wanting to ask you something I can't ask Gemma. There are all sorts of rumours about her and I thought you might know the truth. You know how people talk."

"What sort of rumours?"

"Well, we all know she's eighteen on Saturday. People are saying she'll get all her parents' money then, that she'll be stinking rich."

"You can tell *people*," he stressed the word, feeling irritated, "that they are way off-beam. Gemma's money is tied up until she's twenty–one."

"Ah." Sam hesitated and then went on resolutely, "D'you think … that it'll make her… that we'll … be different?"

Michael was caught off-guard by Sam's straight question, and a chill finger touched him. He knew it would make a difference; it had to do that, money always did. A rich Gemma would be a different Gemma. The finger pressed harder.

He was doing his very best to push his own stab-bing disappointment away from him. He certainly didn't like the thought of "people" gossiping about it.

"So?" he said rather coldly, raising his eyebrows.

"So nothing really," Sam replied, a bit abashed

by Michael's expression. An awkward silence fell between them.

Gemma stood in the doorway and surveyed them.

"What's the matter?" she asked. "Faint from hunger, can't lift a finger?"

Sam and Michael started and automatically looked a bit guilty.

"Tin opener, baked beans." She put them in front of Michael. "Saucepan." She pointed at it. "Eggs." She opened the fridge. She held her breath a little when she did this now, the episode with the rat had left its mark.

"Frying pan, fish slice, Sam." Each thing was placed in front of him. "Oh, and bacon."

The boys rose obediently.

"Wait a minute." Michael put the baked-bean tin down and folded his arms. "I thought men were supposed to be equal, not slaves to your bidding!"

"Do you or do you not want to eat this apple crumble that I spent all last night baking?" Gemma produced it from a cupboard.

"You sure know how to squeeze a fellow," Sam groaned loudly and they both went into exaggerated action.

Gemma was laughing at their absurd pantomime when Rebecca came in, her red-brown curls tied with a pink day-glow ribbon in a sort of fountain over one ear. She was wearing an electric blue T-shirt with a designer slogan printed across it in orange. It always took her twice as long as Gemma to dress.

Michael's inner tension relaxed into this moment of friendly warmth. He stirred the large pan of beans, glad to feel his old group of friends around him.

Sam, too, as he broke the second egg yolk in the pan, watching the yellow spread unbidden over the hot oil, silently hoped nothing would change them. That nothing would change Gemma. He, for one, wouldn't change, he knew how he felt about her. He was relieved she wouldn't have all her inheritance for another three years. Time to breathe in, he reflected.

But their peace didn't last. A motorbike's roar came to a halt in front of the Old Rectory and a helmeted figure dismounted to open the gate and push the bike into the safety of the garden. Then, zippered up to the chin in a shiny leather jacket, the rider walked up the path to the house.

At the sound of the bike, Rebecca looked up. She knew that noise.

"Extra egg needed, Paul's here," she announced.

"Guess who he's come to see, Becca!" Gemma raised her eyebrows at her friend and grinned.

Paul Oliver was a slight, wiry boy who had a bit of a "thing" about Rebecca. He took to turning up wherever she went after school. If they went to the café, he materialized there, too. If she went home, he turned up wanting to know something, or just turned up. At Gemma's it wasn't quite so easy to do this. Even Paul, not the most sensitive of beings, was treading softly with her.

He was in their class, and Rebecca and he acted in

last year's summer play. They shared a love of theatre. He kept on trying to keep her to himself after that. Rebecca, on the other hand, was flattered by his open attentions, but made quite sure she remained part of the wider group. He was a bit of a clown and made her laugh. She liked him, she enjoyed his flamboyance – end of story.

So, by dint of perseverance, Paul made himself part of their circle.

No one noticed that Michael had taken to clamming up when Paul was around. Now, he turned back to the stove, hunching his shoulders a little.

Paul was devoted to his motorbike.

"Friends!" he declaimed with great drama, entering the kitchen with a flourish and waving his helmet. His almost white fair hair was clinging to his head in Roman-like spikes. "A sight to warm my battered soul – to comfort my wounded persona…!"

"Wounded whatsit?" Sam stopped putting knives and forks on the table and snorted. He liked Paul all right, but sometimes he could do without him. This was one of those times.

"Behold!" Paul held out his bike helmet. "If that isn't wounded, I don't know what is!" The helmet's visor was badly cracked

"Ah, met a wall?" Sam was still unsympathetic. All this drama was getting him down.

"I found some low-life playing football with it in the field." This was the playing field at the back of the school.

"Poor Paul, that's rotten." Rebecca, sorry for him, came over to look. "Can you mend it?"

Slightly mollified by her concern, Paul brightened.

"Not a hope," he said almost cheerfully. Then, with an abrupt change of mood, he put the helmet down and went over to Michael, who hadn't looked round. He leaned over his shoulder and watched him spooning the hot beans on to pieces of toast.

"Hi, Mikey. Smells good."

Michael said nothing. His back stiffened slightly.

Rebecca noticed. He's the type to get up Michael's nose, she thought. Michael's not an extrovert.

Paul switched again. With a gesture of high drama he clutched his forehead and, turning to Gemma, exclaimed, "Oh Paul, Paul, manners! Gemma darling, how are you? The Moss birds and Guy the Hulk send love." He kissed her lightly on her cheek and she grinned at him. He was referring to the other half of their group of friends.

Gemma didn't mind Paul. She could take or leave him. He was good-natured, often outrageous, and fun.

"Food, all," she said.

After the meal they relaxed with hot drinks in the sitting-room. Gemma was used to going in there now. Besides, the warm gas fire, looking so like a real open fire, was comforting, even in her centrally heated house.

"I've got an essay to write this evening; looks like I'll be burning the midnight oil if I sit here any longer." Gemma's A-levels consisted of English Literature, Modern History and Economics, a formidable trio.

"Don't mention work in my hearing," Rebecca sighed. "I'm having problems with my problems."

Paul, sitting next to Rebecca on the sofa, said, clutching his heart, or the part of his shirt in that vicinity, "Lady, your problems are my problems!"

Rebecca gave him a shove.

"You think you've got problems…" Michael spread his hands expressively.

Sam looked smug and slightly superior. A-levels were behind him. He'd worry about college when he had to.

"You know," Michael said, looking at Gemma, "Mum's hoping to give you a big firework party on the fifth."

Gemma shifted her position on the sofa; this was an uncomfortable subject.

"She did mention it and it's kind of her, but I've put her off the idea."

"But you love Guy Fawkes', Gem," Rebecca said. "We could let off a few here, in the orchard. We don't have to make a big thing of it."

"No, we don't have to," Gemma's voice was firm, "and we won't. Not this year."

Awkwardness descended on the group, and so did silence.

"Tell you what I'd really like…" Gemma thought she had been too hard on them. They haven't a clue about how I am feeling, she thought, how could they?

"Listen," she went on, "we'll have a little dinner here. We'll get all the gang together, plus a take-away and some really good videos, and have our own do. But no fuss, OK?"

The tension of the moment before broke. Paul was the first.

"Wicked! You can be the hostess with the mostest, and I'll be your—"

"Oh, cut the drama for once!" Sam lost patience with him. Paul made a face.

"Lucy and Tracy will come, of course," Rebecca said, ignoring the exchange. They were twins, the Moss birds Paul mentioned earlier.

"Guy, too." Guy Havant, sometimes known as The Hulk, was in their class and part of their circle, mainly because he hung about with the Moss sisters.

"Fine, just right." Gemma stood up.

"But what about Mum?" Michael was feeling anxious again. "What will she say?"

Gemma paused. "I'll ring her and we'll have a family lunch together. She'll understand."

"Right," Michael said, hoping that would do it.

"Now, I've got to go. See you later."

Gemma left the room and headed for her bedroom.

The watcher outside saw the upstairs light go on. Then made sure that all that could be seen of the back of the Old Rectory was seen. All that could be seen of the watcher, was a white triangle of face with two black voids for eyes, staring steadily out across the orchard. Staring with hatred at the warm glow of light in the kitchen, and the figures moving around inside ... the warmth and the friendship...

Silence fell again after Gemma had gone. Michael leaned over and reached for the TV control.

"OK," said Sam, before he could get to it, "how can we make this dinner special for Gemma?"

"She doesn't want it to be special, that's the point." Why can't they just let things be? thought Michael. Everything is difficult enough as it is.

He watched Paul lean back on the deep sofa cushions, looping his arm over the back as he fiddled with Rebecca's hair ribbon. She shook her head at him and twitched away.

Michael's anxious expression turned darker as he watched him. I hate that creep, he thought suddenly. I wish he was...

"I know!" Rebecca leaned forward eagerly, breaking into his thoughts. "We could play a game. That would make it different. We could play 'Host a Murder', I've always wanted to do that."

"Murder!" Michael exclaimed. "Just what she wants! You really are insane!"

"Listen, Mike, it's only a game. It will be fun, and you can all bring your costumes when you come."

"Our what?" Michael was beginning to feel dizzy.

"It doesn't have to be anything elaborate, just a hat

or something, like charades. It's to set the scene for the game, Murder in the Rectory!" Rebecca threw herself back in her chair, feeling she had explained everything.

"It could be a sort of vicarage meeting or something," she went on vaguely when she saw she hadn't. "We'll think of the characters and plots once we know who's coming. It doesn't need vast numbers, only Gemma's real friends. Tracy and Lucy will love it, it's perfect."

Paul, his mind already engaged with plots and counterplots, clapped his hands.

"Such larks!" he said.

Michael gave in. It was just a game after all, and Gemma might enjoy it. It would certainly mark her day without a big to-do and it was something all of them could give her.

"OK," he said, "we'll have a meeting at my place tomorrow, invent the story and stuff. We'll surprise her. Don't you give the game away, Bec."

"Hey, whose idea was this anyway?" Rebecca threw a sofa cushion at him.

"Shut up, you lot," Sam said. "Action decided. Now I want to watch the film. Switch it on, Mike."

They met at Michael's house as arranged, sitting around the kitchen table.

As it was Saturday, Sam and Rebecca came soon after lunch. Paul wasn't far behind them. He rode up sporting a very expensive, brand new, silver-blue motorbike helmet. The Moss sisters arrived shortly after, delighted with the plan, especially as it involved a bit of drama. Guy tagged along with them.

"I don't care what anyone does as long as I can wear my new dress!" Paul declared before anyone had said a thing, well aware of the reaction he was bound to get. He got it.

Guy sighed heavily and crossed his sizeable arms. His body language said plainly what he thought of Paul in a dress.

Lucy Moss giggled, a little wildly. She fancied Paul, admired his outrageous pranks, and was always trying to attract his attention. Like her sister Tracy she was small and slight and had long blonde hair caught in a low pony-tail down her back. The major difference in the girls' appearance was that Tracy wore her pony-tail high on the point of her crown and it fell straight down over one of her ears. They were both in the school drama group with Paul and Rebecca and had acted in several plays together.

"I'd just love to see you in a micro-skirt, Paulie, knobbly knees and all!" Lucy swung her long hair over one shoulder and bit the end of a strand in excitement.

She's like a firecracker, thought Michael, fizzing away till she explodes. He was too shy to be an actor, but he was always game to do the boring bits for the group, like selling tickets or pinning up posters. They could count on him.

"I'll have you know I have very good legs, Lucy

Moss – want to see?" Paul stood up and began to fiddle elaborately with his belt buckle.

"Oh, sit down and shut up!" Guy, moved to action, stood too, towering above Paul and twice as wide across the shoulders. He couldn't stand all this theatrical rubbish. He wasn't keen on Paul either. He liked him even less knowing that Lucy fancied him. Her vivacity and small, slender form had wound itself around his heart and he would do anything she asked him. She was the main reason that he was there. Of course, he liked Gemma and her crowd, very much, but it was for Lucy that he was putting up with Paul.

Tracy pulled at Guy's rugby shirt. She liked him, and hated to see Paul and Lucy wind him up. He couldn't handle it. She enjoyed acting, too, but, unlike her twin, didn't need to be centre stage all the time.

"Calm down," she said in a voice asking for patience. "This is for Gemma, remember?"

Lucy tossed a coquettish glance at Guy. She knew exactly what effect she had on him. Grinning a little sheepishly at her, he sat down again.

"Got it!" Unabashed, Paul sat too, taking no notice of Guy's interruption. "Forget it's a rectory, right? Let Gemma be the hostess of a glamorous mansion – entertaining a famous crowned head, or head of state, or something like that. There's a murder, and in the party is an equally famous detective, in disguise of course."

"So," Rebecca said, "the unknown murderer kills

the unknown victim and the unknown detective solves the crime?"

"Bull's-eye!" Paul exclaimed. He hadn't thought as far as that, but he was happy to give the impression he had it all worked out.

"We can dole out some cards at the start." Michael was trying to be practical. "So the murderer will know who he is but the others don't. We can all start in different rooms in the house, and have to get ourselves to the safety of the drawing-room, say, without getting killed by whoever is the murderer. He can pounce on anyone he finds."

"Aha, a serial killer on the loose!" Sam was beginning to enjoy himself.

"Only until the first body is found. As soon as that happens we all come together. So we have to find the first victim to protect ourselves from sudden death as well."

"I think I'm lost," wailed Tracy.

"Look," Rebecca said patiently, "it's simple. Number one: the detective has to find the body when he hears the victim scream. Number two: when he finds it, he calls us all in to the murder room from wherever we are in the house. Number three: there he grills us to find out who did it. Number four: we, until we are called by the detective, will be trying to get to the drawing-room to stop being murdered by the murderer who will be still on the loose. Got it?"

Tracy nodded slowly.

"We have to know who the detective is, or he

might get killed, and then where will we be!" A contribution from Lucy.

"Oh, well spotted," said Guy. Lucy preened and looked at Paul.

His bright sharp eyes were switching from face to face. He looks just like a watching bird, thought Tracy. I don't know why Lucy likes him so much. I wouldn't trust him further than I can see. He blows any which way with the wind, always watching for the main chance.

Rita, with armfuls of shopping in supermarket bags, came through the back door.

"Having a conference?" she asked, greeting them and putting the bags down on the worktop.

"Hi, Mum," Michael grinned at her. "In a word, yes."

"Don't mind me," she said with a smile back, "I'll be out of here soon."

"OK." Michael took charge again. He drew a sheet of paper and a biro towards him. "There are eight of us. Gemma, as Hostess, can be told about her character at the time, it's a surprise, right? We all arrive in character with a view to celebrating this visiting bigwig. We then dole out cards, marked for both the murderer and the detective. Everyone else gets a card with nothing on it. We can plan who each of us is in the game now, and where we kick off from. The detective will have to give up his character when we find out who he is on the night."

"Great stuff!" Rebecca's eyes were sparkling. "I'm

for the kitchen, I could be the waitress handing round the drinks, or even the cook!"

There were shouts of, "Bigwig done to death by cooking!" And, "International incident starts in kitchen!"

Michael, biro poised, called order. "Seriously, folks, let's plan, OK?"

6

"We'll have a glass of wine before they arrive," Gemma said. The girls were in the drawing-room in front of the fire. The take-away was in the oven and everything was ready.

It was impossible to ignore the fact that it was bonfire night. Rockets and bangers were going off all round the Old Rectory.

Rebecca looked like a firework herself. She wore scarlet leggings and a tight velvet top in some silvery material. It was stretchy and caught the light when-ever she moved. She had woven pieces of tinsel into her hair.

Gemma thought at first she would wear her black jeans and big midnight-blue sweater, something dark and not at all festive. But when she had gone up to change she found herself taking her new dress out of the wardrobe. It was the one she and her mother picked out for what was going to be this special night. Made of red crushed velvet, in some lights it looked a deep crimson, while in others it glowed scarlet.

"It makes the rest of you look like a wonderful ice-cream," she heard her mother say, that day when Gemma first held it against herself and looked in the mirror. The crimson and scarlet lights threw Gemma's pale creamy skin and ice-gold hair into stark relief.

Gemma had drawn the dress over her head and spun around, making the folds swish and shimmer.

"A raspberry ripple," she said happily, "good enough to eat!" and they both laughed.

Gemma firmly shrugged off the crowding memories and sipped at her glass of white sparkling wine. The front door bell rang so loudly it nearly exploded.

Rebecca, with a wild "It's only them, don't worry!" rushed to open it and the six conspirators tumbled into the hall.

Rebecca returned to Gemma.

"I think you'd better sit down and keep calm," she said. "Your guests have arrived.

Bewildered, Gemma sat.

They came in one by one and Rebecca introduced them.

"The Reverend Meanwell, sanctimonious church-man, friend of the Fullbag family. That's your family, Gem."

Michael entered, collar turned round and dressed

in a pair of black trousers and a black pullover. He walked over to Gemma and kissed her hand.

"Dear lady," he said.

"Mr Fullbag, host of this party and husband to yourself," Rebecca intoned.

Sam came in next, dressed in his father's three-piece suit and sporting a false moustache. He tried to look pompous, and approached Gemma to give her a whiskery kiss, but chickened out, and clearing his throat loudly to cover this, he patted her on the shoulder and took up a Napoleonic pose, hand on breast.

"Lady Feather and her brother, Lord Fuss, guests of quality."

"Lucy!" Gemma smiled, recognizing Lucy Moss as Lady Feather in spite of granny glasses, a flowing scarf and hair stuffed into a pudding-bowl hat. She was foxed for a moment by the slender man standing next to her. He wore brown trousers, and was swamped by a too-large blazer, with a full false beard and moustache.

Then she realized it was Tracy.

Gemma had no idea what on earth was going on, but whatever it was, it was beginning to be funny. She got the giggles.

"Mr Gutt," announced Rebecca. "Spelled with two t's. VIP, bigwig extraordinaire."

Guy Havant, pride of the football pitch, resplendent in a sweatshirt stuffed with an enormous belly, waddled into the room. He lined up with the others, looking decidedly embarrassed. After all, he was a sportsman, not a flipping actor. His face seemed to be trying to convey this.

Gemma doubled up.

"Just call me Angela, darling."

Paul slinked into the room before Rebecca could announce him. He was a wonderful vision in a scarlet satin dress that was a bit too long for him. He had to hold it up with one hand to manage his gliding walk. With it he wore black elbow-length gloves and what looked like a real crocodile handbag hung from his arm.

"I don't know who this is," Rebecca said, hands on her hips and looking slightly annoyed. "He's right off the wall. I thought he was going to be Mr Gutt's security man, Sid Savage."

"I am, darling." Paul leered at Guy who screwed up his face in what looked like pain. "In disguise, of course. I'm the best in the business."

His short blond hair was completely covered with a turban, Carmen Miranda style. Three cherries and a plastic banana hung rakishly off it over one eye. He patted it.

Tears of laughter were rolling down Gemma's cheeks.

"You've been robbing your poor mother's dress shop, Paul Oliver," she gasped.

Rebecca folded her arms and glared at him.

Paul looked crestfallen. He had done all this to impress her.

"More like the school's property cupboard," said Michael. "Exhibitionist!" His tone was sharp.

When Gemma got her breath back she gasped, "You didn't walk here like that, did you, Paul?"

With one voice the others answered for him.

"He did," they said grimly.

"My secret lover," Paul cooed and draped himself over Tracy who flinched. He was having a whale of a time, loving every minute.

"Sorry, love," Paul went on in character to Lucy, who wished it had been her. She thought Paul's performance was wonderful and would have loved it if he was draped round her. "I know he's your husband, darling," Paul went on maliciously, knowing exactly what he was doing, "but he's irresistible!"

Tracy pushed him.

Rebecca, ignoring Paul, dived into a basket and produced several highly coloured scarves and strings of beads. She wound the scarves round her head and shoulders and threw the beads around her neck. They landed on her bosom and fell down to her waist in a clattering jumble. Then she clipped a pair of outrageous earrings on her ears.

"Madame Crystal, Medium of the Minute," she declared. "Mr Gutt does not move a step without me. My predictions are always corrrrect," she announced, rolling her r's in what she hoped was a continental and mysterious way.

"You, Gemma," she said to her amazed friend, "are our hostess, The Honourable Mrs Fullbag, rich as Croesus and worried to death. It's a great responsibility having such a bigwig under your roof."

Rebecca handed her an improbably long cigarette holder. Gemma took it gingerly.

"We have come, dear Madam," Michael stepped forward and clasped his hands together, "to eat and relax together, to give this poor o'er stressed celebrity rest and succour..." He had practised this little speech at home, overcoming his nerves.

Madame Crystal rummaged in her basket again and produced some cards and an old-fashioned alarm clock. She began to hand the cards round the motley company.

"Whoever gets the Ace of Clubs is the murderer," she said. "No peeking... Who's the detective? Ah, I'm not. It's the one with the King of Hearts."

"That's me," said Michael with some relief, he could drop the vicar now. "I wait in the drawing-room until someone screams."

Rebecca explained the game to Gemma.

"You all know your rooms," she said. "We planned all that at Michael's house, Gemma. You're in the dining-room. I'll give everyone ten minutes by this alarm clock to get settled. It'll be in the hall, it's very loud so you'll all hear it. At the scream you try to find the victim, or seek sanctuary. If the murderer gets to you before you get there, tough. The detective then has to deduce who the murderer is when he's got you all together. He can do it any way he likes after he finds the victim.

"Let's go, and remember, all lights off and no one turns one on, OK?"

The watcher didn't see the lights in the Old Rectory go off one by one. The watcher who wasn't outside any more remained a watcher. But the view was much narrower now. All that could be seen was, for the moment, dark and silent. It was just a case of watching ... and waiting...

Leaving Michael sitting in front of the drawing-room fire, the others scattered. The plan was to play the game, eat the meal and then watch videos.

Gemma walked to her place in the dining-room on the other side of the hall and sat on one of the chairs around the large polished table. The game came as a complete surprise and she felt a bit odd, sitting alone in the dining-room. But she was touched by the way her friends had arranged it as a surprise for her.

She could hear the old house creaking as people moved about above her. One especially loud crack seemed to be there in the room with her and she looked nervously over her shoulder. It was pitch dark. But only the heavy curtains hanging in their familiar place over the large windows were there. Nothing else.

Gemma sat twiddling her symbol of an opulent hostess, the cigarette holder. She did not feel at ease. It was all so bizarre, and she was beginning to get one of her headaches. My bag's upstairs, she thought. If

I rush now I could get a tablet before the alarm goes off.

She made the decision and moved quietly into the dark hall. Dim street light filtered through the fan light of the front door, and nearby a rocket burst somewhere with a bang and a hiss. The staircase was lit in sharp relief for a second. Gemma, grateful for the momentary light, shot up the stairs.

7

Rebecca stood in the games-room. The snooker table was shrouded in night and she couldn't even see the dartboard.

Total darkness.

Swathed in her shawls and scarves and hung about with beads that clattered and jangled as she moved, Rebecca realized that she didn't have the costume for secrecy. She would be heard coming a mile off. She grinned in the dark. Good thing she wasn't the murderer then.

She wondered who was. I must make a plan, she thought. I'm Madame Crystal, me, Medium of the Minute. I must get to that body before anyone else if I'm to show off my superior powers. Why did I leave my crystal ball at home, I wonder? Well, never mind, I'll just have to go into a trance and find out that way!

She heaved herself, beads rattling, on to the edge of the snooker table and closed her eyes. Getting into character was what she really enjoyed.

That automatically made her think of Paul. In the darkness Rebecca pressed her lips together. He was trying to get a bit too close for comfort; she didn't find him so amusing any more. She'd have to do something about it.

Propping herself on her elbow and drawing her legs on to the table, she sighed.

This is for Gemma, she told herself. She hoped that Gemma was having fun…

In the Old Rectory's gracious drawing-room, Michael shifted restlessly. Rich Persian rugs lay glowing in the firelight on the polished floorboards. Curtains, draped and looped, hung over the French windows leading to the garden. They cut out any light coming from the fireworks in the sky around.

Outside the room, behind heavy panelled doors, lay the hall with its sweeping staircase. Beside the newel post stood a table holding a telephone, the usual address books and Mrs Jenkins's bowl, no longer of roses, but full of scarlet beech leaves and chrysanthemums. It also held the alarm clock. Michael could hear it ticking through the door.

He got up and began pacing the room with his hands behind his back. What a vicarish thing to do, he thought. I must remember I'm the detective. Ten minutes seems far too long.

He was starting to have doubts about the game. Was it really something Gemma would enjoy? Michael's unhappiness suddenly returned in full. If it wasn't for Gem, he thought miserably, I'd take off – get out. But she needs me ... at least I think she does...

He must try to last out till he heard that scream.

His eye came to rest on something lying on the floor near the door. When he picked it up he recognized it as part of the bunch of plastic fruit that Paul had stuck on his turban.

Blast, Michael thought. Paul would be bound to notice he'd lost part of his head-dress and come looking for it. It would be just like him to think of his appearance first, and wreck the game by coming downstairs just as the alarm went off. Then they would all have to begin again!

I might have time to get it to him, I know where he is, he thought. It'll give me something to do, I'm getting the jitters waiting here.

He opened the door and his long legs took the stairs two at a time. He reached the landing and paused. It was very dark.

It was darker still in the passage and it made him slow down further. He went the rest of the way carefully, feeling the wall. Paul was in the spare room and Michael prepared to give him a nasty surprise.

He opened the door softly and at the same time he whispered in a sibilant, and what he hoped was a ghostly sort of voice, "A present for Angela, with love!"

Then, moving fast, he threw the plastic fruit inside the room. Not waiting for any reaction, he quietly shut the door again and retreated down the passage as fast as the darkness allowed. He didn't hear a sound.

"I'm childish, I know," he grinned to himself. "But I hope he jumped a mile. Slimy toad!"

As he turned the corner to go more carefully down the stairs, he thought he heard a door open at the other end of the passage. It was Gemma's room. He flattened himself against the wall as Gemma scooted past him on her way back to her position in the dining-room.

Michael glided softly back to his post.

Sam's moustache tickled and the cellar was deadly cold. He was glad to have his father's old Harris-tweed three-piece on. He kept trying to peer at his watch to see how much longer he had to stay freezing to death, but couldn't make out the dial in the darkness.

If I was sensible, he thought with grim humour, I'd crack open some of these priceless bottles and sample a few to keep the cold out!

He was impressed with the racks full of wine. He had managed to see them in the moments before he had to turn off the light. They lay in their named and numbered places gathering a crust of romantic grime and showing off their vintage years.

Bet there's a fortune here, Sam muttered. Wish I

was Gemma's husband in real life, I'd be in the gravy all right! Don't suppose I'd appeal to her as Mr Pompous Fullbag though … and in real life…

Gemma's smooth, gleaming head and her delicate oval face rose before him in the darkness and he sighed. It would, he discovered with a small jerk of surprise, be impossible to think of his life without her. When had she become more than just a good friend of his, and best mate of his sister? Sam didn't know.

Suddenly, he passionately hated the money she possessed. She probably wouldn't have looked at him anyway, easy going, good for a laugh Sam, but now she was going to be rich … forget it!

He sat down on the bottom cellar step with a sigh. When would that alarm go off?

Tracy Moss, alias Mr Fuss, wished she hadn't decided to be a man and wear this exceedingly rough and spiky, hairy beard–cum–moustache. It was really daft of her when she was inclined to get skin rashes easily.

I'll be the next best thing to a beetroot tomorrow, she thought dolefully.

She had been allotted the kitchen as her starting place and now stood in the centre of it surrounded by the wonderful smells of the Thai take–away coming from the oven.

She nibbled a crust of French bread that was lying on the kitchen table.

Rebecca had drawn them into Gemma's circle

because they all had a lot of interests in common. Gemma and Sam were not as keen on acting as the other four were, but they made a good back-up team when there was anything going on. Sam was a reliable stage manager on one or two shows, and Gemma was happy to prompt or see to the front of house, both important roles in a production. This common interest bound them all together in a loose, happy group.

Guy had rather barged his way in, following Lucy blindly. But once there, they enjoyed his large presence. Lucy knew he was devoted to her. Tracy thought she treated him badly, and tried to make up to him for it. With Guy they formed a little trio of their own, a sort of satellite, sometimes touching Gemma's larger world, and sometimes just circling round on their own.

Lord Fuss and Lady Feather had been her idea.

Paul was the link. He flitted backwards and forwards between the two groups of friends. Tracy, if she was honest, really didn't trust him. There was something about him that made her feel he needed to know all one's secrets. That he'd dig and dig until he had them, and then... Tracy shrugged her shoulders at herself. Oh! Hurry up, alarm clock, I want to do some prowling...

Guy Havant sat on the edge of the bath. He was not comfortable as it was one of those old-fashioned baths with no surround or panelling, but stood firmly on four curved feet in the shape of lion's claws in the centre of the room.

He tried to sit on the basket-weave chair beside the bath, but the arms of the chair were so close together he couldn't get his extra-stuffed bulk into in. It was touch and go whether he could have fitted it without the extra stuffing.

I wouldn't be here, he thought dismally, if it wasn't for how I feel about Lucy.

Slender and slightly fey, she had totally captured him. Sure, he liked Gemma and her set, they could be fun, and Sam was even known to kick a ball. Michael was no use there, far too long and thin, no force to him. But he had hung about them until the Moss sisters had sort of adopted him. He liked the way they clung on an arm each side of him as they went about together. It made him feel – well – good.

But, if he had his way, Paul Oliver would even now be impaled on the spike on the top of the town-hall roof. Everyone could see that Lucy fancied him. She made no secret of it. What she saw in that weedy ferret of a man, Guy couldn't imagine.

The exhibition he made of himself coming here! In a dress, for goodness' sake! With that … thing on his head. It was all Guy could do to stop himself stuffing that banana…

Guy sat on the edge of the bath and steamed at the memory.

There was only one redeeming thing in it all and that was that Paul was not smitten with Lucy at all –

that showed the sort of fellow he was. He was following Becca Peel around.

Well, as far as he was concerned, when that alarm bell went he'd make a beeline for the drawing-room, and if the murderer got in his way – whoever it was – they would find him a difficult corpse to deal with...

The watcher tensed. It wouldn't be long now. Strong fingers folded into fists. It was hard not to breathe too loudly ... not to get too excited...

Paul opened the Rectory's spare-bedroom door and glanced approvingly at what he could discern of its size and furnishings. He was sorry that neither Gemma nor Rebecca had allowed the use of either of their rooms in the game. He would have loved to see them and done a bit of poking around in their private things. You never knew what you might find out.

This room was at the far end of the landing and the longest walk to the family bathroom. It was OK. He was planning on finding Rebecca first, even if she was the murderer.

Hitching up Angela's skirt he made for the bed. A mirror on the dressing-table took up his movements as he walked across the room. It handed them back to the full length one on the large old-fashioned wardrobe door. Light as Paul was, the old floorboards of the house shook a little with his weight and the wardrobe door, slightly ajar, quivered.

He was very pleased with his performance so far. Guy's expression on the walk over was worth every minute. He chuckled at the memory. A right thicko, Guy. Lucy would never look at a solid lump like that!

Well, it wouldn't do to go off half-cocked, that wouldn't get Rebecca to notice him. Slyly he thought of Lucy's admiration and basked in it a moment before discarding it with a shrug.

Rebecca was the girl for him. He loved her size and her exuberance. He wasn't very tall, he knew, but wasn't there such a thing as attraction of opposites? She just needed a little pressure put on her ... he knew just how to do that now – thanks to Lucy Moss! Paul grinned to himself in the darkness. He had made a start on Rebecca – pressure in the right places, he knew already, always paid off in the end.

God, how the turban itched! Paul pulled it off his head and ran a hand through his sweaty hair that was sticking to his skull like a cap.

His turban rolled to the edge of the bed and as he grabbed it before it fell off, he realized that his three cherries and a banana were missing. Paul cursed quietly, they were his best bit – his *pièce de résistance*. He slid off the bed and got down on his hands and knees to look for them...

"Of all the spooky places this one takes the biscuit!" Lucy spoke aloud and pushed her granny glasses down her nose to see over the top. "A hardened murderer like me won't flinch, though!" She giggled a little.

The Old Rectory attic, deep in inky gloom, was lined with shadowy shapes and forms. They could be anything, draped as they were in dust sheets and curtains, not to mention cobwebs.

Lucy was too excited to feel the cold in the unheated attic. If she shivered it was because of anticipation for the fun to come. She took off her shoes, realizing she had to be absolutely soundless in her role. It was going to be difficult, surprising the others. How will I murder them? she wondered happily.

I'll get Paul first. Her eyes sparkled at the wonderful thought of going silently into where he was, creeping up behind his unsuspecting form and sliding her hands round his throat. I'll whisper, "Die for me, Paul…" in his ear and he'll have to. The thought was delicious, she couldn't think beyond it.

For a moment her good feelings took a check. She knew that Paul would prefer it if Rebecca did that to him. She couldn't hate Rebecca, exactly, she was too nice, too much fun, but she was glad she had been able to tell Paul something secret about her She had hoped that it would put him off her, but it hadn't.

He liked secrets like that, he collected them. Once, when he was in a very showing off mood, after the first night of that play they'd all been in last year, he'd told her he knew a real secret about somebody else. He didn't tell her who or what it was about, not then, but she knew he would. It was only a question of time. Just last week, he had whispered a name in her ear and she knew what he meant. He said, if she did everything he told her, she would know the whole story. He made her promise not to tell a soul, and she wouldn't, of course.

Down in the hall the alarm clock rang. Its bell was so loud and fierce that it nearly fell of the table, but up in the attic it sounded like some far off doorbell.

Lucy, hoping she could imitate a shadow, took a deep breath and opened her door...

Outside the house, the dark sky split and shattered with many distant fireworks. The smell of wood smoke from bonfires drifted over the roofs and through the orchard. In other gardens in the suburbs, there was laughter and noise as Guy Fawkes met his fiery death over and over again.

It seemed darker than ever in the Old Rectory's spare room. Only by some reflected glow from the mirror on the dressing table and the full length mirror on the open wardrobe door, could one see the secondary glow of red stretched across the floor. The mirrors picked up the colour and held it because it wasn't moving. Nothing moved.

Three minutes later the murderer opened the bedroom door and crept silently into the room.

*   *   *

One second later there came the sound of a body tripping over something, and falling on to the floor with a heavy crash.

Thirty seconds later someone screamed and went on screaming.

8

Guy flung himself in through the spare-room door and switched on the light.

Lucy was too hysterical to notice anything. Her hat was off and so were her granny glasses. Her mouth was open as wide as it was able to go, allowing the terrible screams she was making to leave it.

The sudden glare of the overhead light dazzled Guy's eyes, but he saw, in that first glance, a sight that he knew he would never forget.

Paul. He lay on his back on the carpet beside the bed. His legs were tangled up in the red satin dress which forced his knees to lie on one side at an unnatural angle. His head was close to the wardrobe door. This was open, swinging very slightly, on its hinges.

Paul wasn't moving.

Guy was so shocked that he couldn't take in the full horror of the scene. All he was conscious of was that Paul was lying still, and there was something very odd about his head.

But he didn't stay to look closer. His first thought was for Lucy. She was sitting against the bedroom wall with her legs pulled up tight against her chest. She was pressing herself against the wall, trying to push herself as far away as she could from the dreadful figure on the floor.

Lucy's screams slammed into Guy's head; he had to stop them. Instinctively, he bent over the crouching girl and lifted her up bodily in his strong arms. He had to get her away from there and out into the passage.

Just as instinctively, her hands left her face and held on around his thick neck. She buried her head into his shoulder and, mercifully, her screams dwindled to sobbing and then to hiccuping moans.

"What's happened to Lucy?" Michael was belting up the stairs two at a time. Rebecca was not far behind him. The screams sounded real.

Guy opened his mouth but no words came out. All he could do was jerk his head in the direction of the open door.

Michael went past him, saw Paul and froze. With immense presence of mind he turned to Rebecca and put his arm across the doorway, blocking her entry.

"Call an ambulance, Bec. Something's happened

to Paul," he said. Her first thought was to keep on going, to rush in and see for herself, but Michael's arm was like rock barring her way. She looked at his face, white and set, and turned to do what he said.

"Becca, call the police too, OK?" He was trying to steady his voice. He had seen, in that single moment, what was wrong with Paul's head. He had seen the plastic bag.

"Becca!" he almost shouted after her. "Go to Gemma, stay with her. Whatever you do, don't let her come up."

Guy had found his voice.

"I'll take Lucy downstairs and stop the others."

Too late, Tracy, whipping off her beard, was trying to hug what she could reach of Lucy, frantically asking what was wrong with her sister.

"She's OK." Guy was trying to calm Tracy down. "We'll take her into Gem's room, that will be easier. Which is it, do you know?" They disappeared into one of the doors on the landing.

Michael could hear Rebecca's voice on the stairs, raised and shrill as she urged Sam to return to the drawing-room. He heard footsteps receding, and then heard Rebecca reach the phone in the hall and dial.

He went swiftly back to Paul. With part of his mind shocked into numbness, he knelt beside him and undid the string that was tied tightly round his neck, fixing the plastic bag firmly in place. It was a large pedal-bin liner, white and strong. The police didn't like anyone to touch the body, he knew, but Paul might still be alive, he had to do this.

He pulled it away from where it was clinging to the damp face, shuddering as he made the stronger tug to get it away from Paul's nostrils. Condensation smeared the inside of the bag and lay in a fine wet layer over Paul's head. His face was very white, with red blotches around his nose and cheeks. Michael could see that he wasn't breathing any more, that the dampness was the result of his last desperate breaths.

Kiss of life? Michael had heard that someone who had stopped breathing could be brought back by it. But he didn't know what to do. He racked his brains. Tracy knows, he thought, she went to first aid classes once when she needed to know about it for a play they were doing. But this was for real. How could he ask Tracy to come and do it now? He had to try. He struggled to remember all the films he had seen when someone was given the kiss of life. Screwing up his courage he forced himself to touch Paul's face. It was still warm and this gave him the strength to pinch his nose and force open his mouth. Leaning down to cover it with his own was the hard bit. But Michael managed it and blew deeply down into Paul's stretched mouth.

He did this until the deep breaths he took made him giddy and he had to stop. Paul hadn't moved.

Michael heard a gasp and someone came to kneel beside him. It was Gemma.

"My God, Mike, how dreadful," she whispered.

"Becca told me she thought something serious had happened to Paul, and you didn't want me to see. I wasn't going to leave you here alone, no matter what. But Mike, Paul's ... dead, isn't he?"

9

Police and ambulance sirens sounded together and the flashing headlights from the vehicles told of the speedy arrival of both. Rebecca was watching for them and opened the front door at once.

The professionals streamed in and were directed up the stairs.

Badly shocked and afraid, Rebecca and Sam watched a folded stretcher being lifted over the banisters. A female police officer paused in the hall and looked at their scared faces. She also noted their unusual clothes.

"Been having a party?"

There seemed to be no answer to that.

"We'll wait for them in the kitchen, shall we?" The police woman spoke more kindly, but still with authority. "It's more comfortable there, I'm sure. Perhaps, a pot of tea?"

Rebecca saw the sense in this and led the way, unwinding her scarves and untangling the many necklaces as she did so.

The WPC noticed Guy and the two sisters standing in an uncertain huddle at the top of the staircase. "Come and join us," she said, "I don't suppose we'll have long to wait. The chief inspector will want to speak to you all."

Statements, they learned, were to be taken by Chief Inspector Beale in the dining-room.

Paul's body was carried out, when photographs had been taken and the medics satisfied, to the waiting ambulance. The group of frightened teenagers did not see it go, but they heard the front door slam and the ambulance drive away. The feeling of unreality that hung over the group since the body was discovered, hardened into fact with its departure.

Chief Inspector Beale, in charge of the investigation, addressed them in Gemma's kitchen.

"Paul Oliver is dead," he told them. "Someone has killed him. Even if it could be supposed that he had tied the bag over his head himself, he could hardly have been responsible for the colossal blow on the back of his head that laid him out first."

He was a small, rather round man with a shock of grizzled hair that fell down boyishly over his forehead. But there was nothing boyish about his grey eyes as he looked round the shocked group.

"You will each tell me," he said with quiet authority, "what you were doing, and where you were at the time of this murder, for that is what it is. No one is going home before that is done."

He then took up his position in the dining-room, sitting on one side of the large, polished table, and summoned Gemma in first. He was gentle with her. He had known her parents well. They were good community people, generous with their time and money, and were sorely missed. This tragedy, following on their sudden death and involving their only daughter, was appalling.

"So, it's your birthday today, Gemma?" he began.

Gemma nodded.

"And this party was a surprise for you?"

"Not the party," Gemma told him. "Just the game." Inwardly, she flinched. It had *started* as a game.

Questioned about her movements she confessed she had dashed upstairs sometime during the allotted ten minutes.

"I went for my painkillers, I had a headache."

"Did you see anyone?" Chief Inspector Beale asked her.

"No one. All the doors were closed, and everything was dark."

Gemma suddenly remembered the drawing-room door; it had been open a little when she came downstairs, or so she thought.

The chief inspector caught the flicker of uncertainty in her eyes.

"And?" He tried to prompt her. But Gemma had

decided that she wasn't sure about the door, and shook her head.

"That's everything I can think of," she said.

"Is there anything you can tell me about Paul Oliver, Gemma? Did he have any enemies?"

Gemma was uncertain what to say. She knew that not everyone liked Paul. But not liking someone was not a reason to kill them.

She shook her head. "No," she said simply.

"Nothing else?"

Gemma hesitated. There was something else she'd like to tell him, but it wasn't about Paul. He prompted her.

"It's just that ... when I came home first, after the ... after Mum and Dad were killed..." She swallowed, feeling something sticking in her throat.

The inspector quietly waited for her to go on.

"I ... we, Sam, Michael, Becca and me, found a dead rat in the fridge." She said this in a hurry, it sounded so very unlikely, but she hadn't been able to forget it.

"Did you now?" Gemma was relieved that he seemed to take it seriously for she was struggling with a wild desire to laugh. Hysteria, she said to herself, biting her lip.

"And do you think it has something to do with Paul's murder?"

Under control again, Gemma said, "No ... I don't know what to think about it. I've tried to forget it, but I thought ... well, I thought ... I'd tell you."

"I'm glad you did."

Inspector Beale dismissed her courteously, saying that he would want to talk to her again.

Guy came in.

The inspector looked at his large, muscular frame and square, open face. He wondered what this boy could have had in common with Paul Oliver; he didn't look the theatrical type.

Guy told him how he rushed in and took Lucy away from the room where she found Paul's body. The way he spoke about his concern for the shocked girl made the policemen suspect his feelings for her.

"Did you like Paul?" he asked bluntly.

Guy's face went dark red. He pulled a meaty hand through his hair. He had despised Paul. How could he say that?

"He's … all right." He thought if he said it very fast it would sound like the truth.

"Did you approve of him dressing up as a girl?" The inspector wouldn't let him off the hook.

"Well … it's a bitofalaugh," Guy mumbled into his sweatshirt.

"I see." Inspector Beale raised an eyebrow. He had his answer. Odds on Guy couldn't stand Paul.

However, his thoughts went on. He's such a big, beefy fellow, if he wanted to kill Paul Oliver, he just had to pick him up by his neck and shake him, he wouldn't bother with a plastic bag.

To Guy's relief, he changed tack.

"Did you see or hear anything at all while you were

waiting in the bathroom before the scream?"

Guy thought hard.

"I think I heard a door open and close once. I was fed up with waiting, so I put my head out to see who it was."

"Who was it?"

"It was all so dark, and whoever it was went fast. It was difficult to be sure."

"Male or female?"

"Well," Guy's forehead wrinkled with the effort of thought, "I think the door was Gemma's room. We took Lucy in there and it's opposite the bathroom. But the figure could have been either, it was like a shadow."

"Let us know, Guy, if you have any other thoughts about this, won't you?"

Guy nodded, very thankful that the questioning was over and he could go.

Tracy and Sam soon told their stories. Theirs were simple. They had neither heard nor seen anything out of the ordinary while they waited in their separate rooms. Sam could say he liked Paul, so could Tracy. If either of them had reservations, they kept them to themselves. Neither of them could think of any enemies he might have had.

Lucy followed Sam.

"So you drew the murderer's card, Lucy Moss. And you were waiting in the –" the inspector looked at his notes – "attic?"

Lucy's sobs broke out again.

Inspector Beale realized he had not been very tactful. Poor little thing, he thought. She drew the murderer's card and was the one to find the body. That was a bit crude of me.

He sent the constable who was sitting further along the table, taking notes of the interviews, to fetch the female police officer from the kitchen. She entered, saw Lucy's shaking shoulders and drew up a chair next to her. She put her arm around her.

"Be brave," she said kindly. "You want to help catch the one who killed Paul, don't you?"

Lucy mopped her face with her damp handkerchief and her sobs subsided into hiccups.

"Now, Lucy," Inspector Beale started again, "tell us in your own words exactly what happened."

Falteringly, Lucy described her wait in the attic until she heard the alarm. She told the inspector how she had gone to the spare room on purpose to find Paul first and how she had tripped over his prostrate body in the dark.

"I ... think I caught my hand on the bedside light and knocked it off as I fell, I know I knocked something." She rubbed at the back of her right hand where an angry bruise was beginning to form.

"Where was it exactly, d'you know?"

"It must have been on the bedside table, I don't know exactly…" she trailed off.

After a slight pause the inspector went on. "What made you go to…" he stopped himself, he nearly said 'murder', "him first?"

Tears began to trickle down Lucy's blotchy cheeks again.

"I … I liked him," she said shakily. "I thought it would be fun."

"Now, Lucy," the inspector said, leaning forward with his arms on the table and speaking softly. "I have to ask you if you know of any reason why someone should do this terrible thing to Paul, any reason at all?"

He had expected her to shake her head, but she blew her nose and said huskily, "Paul told me he knew a … secret about someone…" Her sentence floated in the air.

"Yes, go on. Who, Lucy?"

Lucy cleared her throat. "He made me promise not to tell anyone."

The female police officer took her hand.

"Paul's dead, love. We have to find out everything we can. If you can help us catch his killer, you must say," she said.

Lucy gave a shuddering sigh. She seemed to shrink into the chair.

"I can't say. Ask Michael, he knows…"

Lucy's slight figure began to tremble.

Inspector Beale felt she had said all she could for the moment. She was in shock and in need of a hot sweet drink.

He nodded to the WPC who helped her up and guided her out of the room.

Then it was Rebecca's turn.

"Yes," she told Inspector Beale, "Michael did stop me going any further into the room."

"What did you see, Rebecca?"

"I caught a glimpse of the body, but only up to the waist."

"And did you think then that Paul was dead?" The inspector was keen to know what had been passing through her mind at that moment.

"No, not dead!" It hadn't occurred to Rebecca that he might have been lying there lifeless.

"So what, then?"

"Well…" Rebecca found herself floundering. "Maybe he'd had some sort of accident, or felt faint … but when Michael told me to call the police … I didn't know what to think."

"Tell me, Rebecca," the inspector held her eyes with his and she found herself unable to look away.

"You knew Paul Oliver well, is there anything at all that you know about that would account for him dying like this?"

Tears rose to Rebecca's eyes and she willed them to stop there. She was feeling unbearably miserable and guilty. Guilty because she knew Paul really fancied her and she took it all so lightly, like a bit of a joke. But he had meant it and she hadn't brushed him off as she should have done.

She knew now that was a mistake. After what he had tried to do, only yesterday, she was definitely going to end it. Now he was dead. But nothing he had done was bad enough to make someone kill him, was it? I'm hesitating too long, she thought, panicking slightly.

"No one's perfect," she said at last. "He didn't deserve this."

The inspector looked at her distressed, intelligent face and wondered what she had left out. He sighed.

"OK, only one more of you to see. Would you call Michael Palmer, please?"

Chief Inspector Beale looked closely at the tall, pale boy who now stood in front of the dining table, which was covered with several sheets of paper, statements and notes.

"I believe you were to be the detective in your game?" He lightened his question with a slight smile.

Michael nodded, aware of the irony. It didn't make him feel any better.

"You were stationed in the drawing-room. Did you, at any time during the ten minutes when you all waited for the game to start, leave your position?"

If it was possible, Michael's face grew paler. He was dreading this question. Over and over he had asked himself if Paul had still been alive when he had opened his door a crack to throw his plastic rubbish in. Or could he have prevented the murder, if he had gone in and *given* it to Paul?

He even wondered if he could just say that he hadn't left his post. He didn't think that anyone had seen him. He stammered hopelessly, "No … that is

… not altogether. I mean, I did have to go up once, but I came back again…"

The chief inspector looked at him steadily.

Michael pulled himself together and tried to explain.

"So," Chief Inspector Beale summed up, "you opened the door to the spare room, threw in the plastic fruit, and shut the door again, not saying anything and not seeing anything, and also, not hearing anything.

"I … did say something…"

The chief inspector raised his eyebrows.

"I … sort of whispered."

"What?"

"Here's a present for you, Angela…" Michael hunched his shoulders miserably.

"Meaning the plastic fruit?"

"Yes."

"Not meaning anything else?"

"No."

"Doesn't sound a friendly thing to say?"

Michael couldn't say anything. He hadn't meant to be friendly.

"Did you get an answer?"

"I did it all very fast, I didn't wait."

Inspector Beale allowed a short silence before he began again.

"When you were in the room with the deceased alone, you attempted to give him the kiss of life? Very commendable. You had to remove the plastic bag from over his head to do this?"

Michael nodded again, remembering the clammy, lifeless feel of Paul's face under its skin of moisture. He shuddered.

The policeman still held him in his unblinking gaze.

"Did it ever occur to you that you were disturbing what might have been vital clues to the murderer?"

Michael's distress deepened.

"Look Michael, it was obvious from the position of the body and the way his legs were tangled up in his skirt, that whoever struck Paul had turned him on his back after hitting him and before positioning the plastic bag. It would have been easier to do it that way."

Michael shuddered again, but said nothing.

"Was there anything in the bedroom that struck you as strange or unusual?" the inspector went on.

Michael tried to consider. Everything about that ghastly moment seemed strange and peculiar. All he could remember was the awful plastic fruit lying on the carpet next to Paul's outstretched hand. Had he been about to pick them up? Michael made himself remember.

He said, "The wardrobe door was open, but Gemma says it tends to do that when there's movement in the room. The catch is loose."

"Anything else?"

"No."

"Nothing that might have been used to inflict the blow on the head?"

"I didn't know he had been hit on the head, not then, not until you told us. There was a smear of blood in the bag, but I didn't connect it with a blow at the time. If it was on the back of his head, I couldn't see it. There was nothing that I saw in the room, or on the floor."

"What about the furnishings? Any lamps, that sort of thing?"

"I don't think I know the room well enough," answered Michael. He was puzzled by the question. "I wasn't looking for blunt instruments, if that's what you mean."

Blunt instruments. Suddenly the words triggered something in his memory he had completely forgotten and his eyes widened with the struggle to remember.

He was looking at Paul's plastic-covered head once more, lying on the spare-room carpet. He could even remember the colour of the carpet now: bottle green. He watched himself, as if he was another person, kneel by the body. He saw his hand, the right one, grab something that was lying close to Paul's still head, and push it, with some force, away. It was in his way. He needed the room to get quickly into a position to loosen the plastic bag and he had forgotten all about it. The memories that followed that particular moment were quite enough to blot it out.

The inspector noticed his change of expression.

"Something come back, has it, Michael?"

Michael, experiencing again the shock of it all, was unable to think fast enough. He shook his head.

The inspector's eyes scanned his notes. "Lucy Moss said that when she fell over the body, the back of her right hand caught the lamp on the bedside table, knocking it to the floor. Did you see it there?"

Was it a lamp? Michael, still grappling with his jumbled memories, said nothing.

"It's a wooden lamp-base with a particularly heavy lead foot. PC Jacks found it sticking out from under the bed – the other side. Looked as if it had been thrown there."

Michael shook his head again. A sudden stab of sheer terror paralyzed his train of thought. He wanted to run.

"Well," Chief Inspector Beale smiled at him pleasantly, "forensics will tell us more about that later on, there may be … marks on it."

The significance of what the inspector said finally pierced his numb brain. Fingerprints! Did he mean fingerprints? Oh God, his fingerprints would be on it! What a fool he was, he must tell him – now!

As he opened his mouth to speak the policeman's next question took him by surprise.

"Do you usually carry a handkerchief?"

"Um … well, no," Michael replied, bewildered. He hadn't for years.

"Yet you had one in your pocket tonight?" All their pockets had been turned out earlier on in the investigation.

"I ... I was supposed to be a vicar," Michael hastened to explain. "I borrowed one from Sam, as I thought vicars might use one, to mop their brows, and that..." God, that sounds daft, he thought.

"Not to wipe away fingerprints?"

"No!" Michael said that with more emphasis than he meant. "You see," he stammered desperately, knowing he had to tell the truth and knowing that he should have done so before, as it would seem so lame now. "I think I did see a lamp, or something..."

"Just saw it?"

"Well, I think I may have swept it out of the way before I took the plastic bag off."

Chief Inspector Beale looked at Michael sternly. "Another piece of evidence removed by you. Where was it?"

"It ... it was close against Paul's head. I remember now, I needed the space ... I pushed it away."

"Oh, yes...?" The inspector left the sound of his words hanging in the air, disbelief in every syllable.

His next question came out of the blue.

"Did you like Paul Oliver?" He asked it bluntly.

Michael, still confused and miserable, was caught completely off-guard.

"O-of course. We all did."

Chief Inspector Beale was a practised interrogator. He saw Michael's face close up.

"That isn't what Lucy Moss told me."

"Lucy?" Michael's mind galloped. Oh God, what had Paul told her?

"She said that Paul knew a secret about you. I gathered it was something that you would rather keep hidden."

"She's crazy! She'll say anything. Everyone knows she was silly about Paul."

"Then what would make her say such a thing?"

"Well…" Michael was so obviously floundering. "Perhaps she thinks it might show that he really cared for her … to tell her something like that. He was always making things up – I don't know."

"Or she might have been trying to help us find out why he was killed? What do you think?"

Michael felt as if someone had just thrown icy water in his face. He couldn't speak. Chief Inspector Beale watched him for a long moment.

"Paul Oliver 'cared' for somebody else, didn't he?" He switched back to the previous subject.

Michael found his voice. It felt like someone else speaking.

"Yes. I suppose so … yes, Rebecca." There's no point in hedging, he seems to know everything anyway, Michael thought dismally.

"And Rebecca, who did she 'care' for?"

Michael flinched at the way he said 'care'. It seemed he was trying to belittle his friends' feelings, make them sound shallow. I hate this man, he thought suddenly. His reply came out too loud and full of aggression.

"If Rebecca felt anything for anyone, she didn't tell me," he said and felt his face going red. His eyes suddenly prickled and, to his horror, they began to fill with tears.

The chief inspector stood up.

"That's enough for tonight," he said abruptly. He indicated the door and Michael, somehow, got to his feet.

At the kitchen door, the chief inspector said to the others, "We'll take you all home now. This is a very serious crime, as you know, so I will be wanting to do some more questioning tomorrow.

"We haven't ruled out the possibility of an intruder, but it seems unlikely at the moment. Forensics will be looking at that anyway. All of you, stay home until you hear from me. Gemma, have you anywhere you can go tonight?"

Gemma looked at Rebecca.

"Stay at our place," Rebecca said to her firmly.

Michael wanted to protest, to say that Gemma belonged with him and Rita, but his interview had severely shaken him. He said nothing.

No one else was saying much either. They put on their coats in silence, avoiding each other's eyes. Michael wanted to slink away into the dark. He didn't dare look in Lucy's direction although he desperately needed to know what Paul had told her.

Telling his mother about tonight was going to be very tough.

"I'll ring Rita when I get to Becca's," Gemma said, guessing at Michael's feelings.

She felt a stab of guilt at abandoning him, but at

that moment she wanted to have the closeness of Sam and Rebecca. There was no pressure with them, no family ties. She didn't want to have to cope with that right now.

Anxious and afraid, Michael went home alone.

10

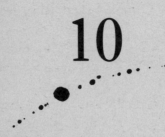

"Oh God, Gemma, they've taken Michael!" Rita's voice on the telephone was almost unrecognizable.

It was twelve o'clock the next day, Sunday morning. Gemma, Rebecca and Sam, looking like three pale ghosts, had just finished a very late breakfast, or what they could eat of it.

Rebecca and Sam's parents were away for the weekend. They had gone to visit Sam and Rebecca's aging grandparents in Devon. Sam, who knew where they would be staying, rang them at first light. He wanted to get to them first, in case the papers mentioned Paul's death. After a bit of a tussle he managed to assure them they should stay there, arguing sensibly there was really nothing they could usefully do at home.

"Michael!" Gemma's eyes swivelled round to look at Rebecca. The phone in the Peel household was in the kitchen, on the cluttered dresser.

Sam, about to wash up, dropped the plates in the sink with a clatter.

"But why?" Gemma asked Rita, feeling dazed. "Why Michael?"

"Please come. I need to see you, Gemma. I don't understand anything – what has been going on?"

"Didn't you get a chance to talk to Michael?"

"He told me such dreadful things about last night … I could hardly take them in. Then the police came to take him for more questioning this morning, I went with him, and he wasn't allowed to leave… Oh Gemma … they took his fingerprints…"

Rita's control broke and Gemma couldn't bear it.

"I'm on my way; hold on, Rita." She put the phone down.

"Listen," she told the others, "I've got to go to her. Michael has been detained. It's a dreadful mistake, but Rita needs me. Tell the police where I am if they want me, won't you?"

"Go," said Rebecca.

Rita's ravaged face shocked Gemma. Usually so together and always in control, she had fallen apart.

"Of course he didn't kill anyone," she tried to comfort the distraught woman. "We all know that. He had no reason, no motive. The police will discover their mistake soon, they must."

Rita tore a piece of paper from the roll on the

kitchen wall and blew her nose. Her red and swollen eyes looked helplessly at Gemma.

"Oh Gemma, it was awful. I was there while they questioned him. We had to get our solicitor, too; he's with Michael now, and he cautioned Michael not to say anything. They tried to make him say he'd done it. That he'd gone up, not just to throw in the plastic things, but to hit Paul on the head and stifle him. That he'd got the bag in his pocket all the time. His fingerprints are on the lamp, you know … the one that was used to…"

Rita broke off to dab at her eyes. "They kept talking about 'opportunity, and motive'."

"What possible motive?" Gemma asked, thinking furiously. Michael was never one of Paul's closest friends, didn't always find him amusing … but this?

"The police searched Paul's house sometime in the early hours. Oh, his poor mother!" Rita took in a deep breath and steadied her voice before she said, "They found a letter among Paul's recent papers. One of those anonymous things, threatening to hurt him. They're trying to link it to Michael. The police have been told that Paul knew some secret about Michael, and that was the motive, to shut him up!"

"Oh, Rita…" Gemma could not find any words to describe how she felt, or to give comfort to her aunt. She only knew Michael was not, *could* not be a killer.

She put her arms round Rita's shoulders and laid her cheek against her aunt's tear-stained face.

"Do you have to go to work this evening?"

Rita sighed. "I must. They're expecting me. And perhaps it'll take my mind off things for a bit. But you could come and stay. They can't keep Michael for ever."

Gemma shook her head. She felt instinctively that when Michael got home that night, he would not welcome any company, not even hers.

"I think I'll ask Becca if she could bear to come back home with me tonight, that is, if the police let us," she said slowly. "It isn't what I really want to do, but you see, if I put off going back, it will be ever so hard to do it later." She gave a slight smile. "Rather like getting back on a horse after a very bad fall."

She expected Rita to protest, so was relieved and a little surprised when she just said, "If that's what you really feel you must do, dear Gemma, then, I suppose you must."

"You'll see," Gemma said, as she kissed her aunt goodbye. "It seems pretty black now, but Michael will be back with us very soon. He didn't do it, and they'll have to let him go. I just know it." She added to herself, "And I'll do everything I can to prove it."

Fine words, she mused on the short journey back to Rebecca's house. Easy to say, but how to do?

Gemma, dreading having to tell the others about Michael, desperately hoped that Rebecca would agree to come home with her. She knew she wouldn't be able to face being there entirely on her own. The question that lay unanswered in her heart was, would she ever?

*   *   *

It was about five o'clock in the afternoon when the two girls stood in the Old Rectory kitchen again. The police had given the house the all clear when Gemma phoned to ask if they could return. Forensics had finished with it.

After Paul's body had gone they had combed through the house, the orchard as well, working through the night. The house had been sealed off during this, with a uniformed policeman standing guard at the door. Now the Old Rectory stood empty again.

The forgotten Thai take-away, still in the oven where it had been left, was now stone cold and beginning to smell sour. The glasses and bottles of wine were standing on the table, waiting for the party that never got going.

The girls cleared away; it gave them something useful to do.

"I'd better ring Mrs Jenkins soon," Gemma said, "to tell her it's OK to come in tomorrow. She probably knows what happened and she'll want me to keep in touch. I'll do it in a minute; let's have some tea first."

Rebecca sniffed the creamy top of a bottle of milk and wrinkled her nose.

"We're going to need some milk; I'll go to the shop," she said, picking up her bag again. "You'll be OK?"

Gemma nodded. She was surprised how easy it

had been to walk into the house. It was, in fact, just like any other time.

Yes, of course she could clearly remember the dreadful events that had ripped their game apart. She could, if she wanted to, hear Lucy scream again and see Paul's still body in her mind. They were awful moments, she'd never forget them, but awful as they were to her, they had not left their mark upon the house. It was still the calm, serene place it had always been.

Gemma let out a long, deep breath.

But everything was a mess! Paul killed, gone for ever, Michael questioned about his murder, and Rita distraught about her only son. More distraught than Gemma had ever seen her.

Needing some space, she unlocked the back door and stepped out into the garden.

The orchard trees were shedding their leaves fast now. They lay in drifts upon the lawn and in soft heaps against their trunks. Some leaves still clung to the blackening branches. We need just one strong wind, thought Gemma, that'll get them all going.

Then something caught her eye, something moving in the longer grass down by the fruit trees. Gemma paused and stared in its direction.

Dusk was falling very quickly; it was almost dark.

There it was again, that movement. Something like a shadow melting into the darkening orchard...

Gemma took some steps toward the edge of the lawn.

"Who's there?" she called out, and then began to be afraid.

There was someone there. She saw a figure detach itself from the gloom and begin to run away in the direction of the old stone wall.

"Stop!" she shouted, fear suddenly gone and anger taking its place. Without pausing further, she belted down the garden, determined to find out who had taken advantage of her empty house and come, perhaps, to rob it.

A slight figure, all in black, was in the process of climbing the stone wall at the bottom of the orchard. It achieved a foothold and in a trice one leg was flung over the wall. The other was about to follow when Gemma caught up. She seized the dangling leg and hung on.

The figure, still fairly obscure from Gemma's angle, kicked out at her to release her hold, but she clung on to it and pulled hard.

"Let go!" a girl's voice shouted. "You'll have me down!"

"I won't let you go. Come down here," Gemma shouted back, not knowing where she got her courage from. She held on to the captured leg grimly.

The other leg came back over the wall reluctantly, and shrugging Gemma off, the girl attempted to leap the distance to the ground. She stumbled a little, falling to her knees as she landed; it was a long drop. Rubbing her right knee, the girl righted herself and stood trying to look defiantly at Gemma.

"Losing a few apples wasn't going to hurt anyone." Her voice sounded resentful and somehow accusing.

Gemma blinked. The fact that the intruder may have been in the garden after harmless apples took her by surprise. Her mind had been running on much more dramatic lines than that.

"You were after apples?"

She studied the girl who stood in front of her. She was standing with her hands on her hips, doing her best to look unruffled. She was not a lot taller than Gemma and was dressed entirely in black. Her white face gleamed in the dimming light, and her dark eyes glittered. They stared unblinking at Gemma from under a thatch of spiky black hair. She wore a shabby denim jacket, black too, which ended at her waist revealing the short, tight skirt she wore below it. So short it nearly disappeared completely leaving her thin legs, encased in black leggings, exposed. As far as Gemma could see, she wore no make-up, but several silver studs gleamed from her ears. Her legs ended with feet encased in much-scuffed heavy black boots. The whole effect was both dramatic, and somehow pathetic.

Gemma noticed that a small hole had appeared in her leggings; she had obviously torn them when she fell.

The girl's expression became a little scornful as she held Gemma's gaze.

"Look on," she said, "it's free!"

"Where d'you come from?" Gemma finally asked.

The girl jerked her head towards the wall. "There."

"But that's just the old churchyard. Come on, where d'you live?"

"I told you. It's a squat, didn't you know?"

"Squat? You mean you've got into the church?"

The girl shrugged. "Not exactly the Hilton, but it's a roof."

Gemma felt suddenly at a loss. In her comfortable existence she had never come face to face with someone who had to look for a roof. The stranger gave her a helping hand.

"You're Gemma, right? My name's Jet."

Gemma was startled. "How'd you know my name?"

The girl, Jet, gave a shrug and a one-sided smile.

"Made it my business. Got to know who your neighbours are, don't you?" Her smile broadened a little. "May be undesirables, right?"

"Jet's an odd name." Gemma thought the strange girl was like some hobgoblin that had materialized out of nowhere.

"Yeah, I like the colour." Jet continued smiling as if everything Gemma said was funny.

"You mean, you changed your name to Jet because you like black?"

"Good enough reason." This was a flat statement.

"Take some windfalls," Gemma said impulsively. "Have as many as you want, most of the apples have dropped by now. Only next time don't come over the wall, come to the front."

Jet looked wary and Gemma realized that she probably wouldn't come to the front. She was reminded of some kind of shy, wild animal.

"I'll get you a bag," she said, and turned to go to the house.

"Thanks."

Jet kept pace with her. At the kitchen door, Gemma stopped. She didn't want to seem ungenerous to this strange waif who had to squat in a deserted church, but she didn't really want her in the house.

"Wait here, I won't be long," she said hurriedly and darted inside.

She was only a moment and Jet didn't move. Darkness had fallen now and a mist was rising from the damp ground, making her shiver in her thin jacket.

"What d'you do for heat in there?" Gemma couldn't help asking as she handed her the plastic bag.

"We got sleeping bags and rugs and that." Jet gave a shrug as if she didn't need anything else. "We also got a primus, we're OK. We spend a lot of time in the caff. It's not for long."

"We?"

"Roach and me."

"Roach?" Another weird name, Gemma thought.

"He's me brother, see, and a bit slow like," Jet went on patiently, seeing Gemma's questioning look.

"Slow, slowcoach – Roach. He wouldn't like it, being called cockroach, so he's Roach. He don't mind that."

The light dawned on Gemma – rhyming slang.

"You're Londoners, then."

Jet grinned again and this time her smile changed her face dramatically. It became friendly and a touch vulnerable.

"Got it in one," she said.

"When did you get here?" Gemma was reminded of the light Rebecca thought she saw in the church, but that was weeks ago.

"Yesterday. We've been around for longer, staying with a mate, but he had to push off. He told us about the squat – used it himself a while back. Anyway, we've got the promise of a place in a couple of weeks."

"Oh good," Gemma said, but she was startled at the thought of the old church being a known squat. How many people had found a sort of shelter in it, just the other side of her orchard wall? she wondered. We were living our lives, warm and well fed, and on the other side of the wall were people without anywhere. It made her feel very small and acutely uncomfortable.

"Why did you leave London?" Gemma was curious.

Jet's face took on a slightly haunted expression.

"I got to go, Roach will wonder," she said. She clutched the plastic bag to her and turned away.

Before Gemma could ask another question, Jet had run away towards the trees.

"Thanks for the apples." Her voice drifted back to Gemma as she disappeared into the misty orchard.

"Who on earth's that?"

Gemma started. Rebecca had returned with a bottle of milk and had come up behind Gemma's shoulder. She caught Jet's last remark and could just glimpse her disappearing back.

"Tell you inside," Gemma replied, "it's cold out here." Bet it's cold in the church too, she thought, and shivered. Her encounter, so unexpected, had unsettled her quite deeply. Apples, windfalls at that, were a small offering from one who had so much, to one who had very little.

"Tea?" asked Rebecca, looking into her friend's preoccupied face. "Or your usual?"

Gemma sighed and let Jet go.

"Tea, workman's brew," Gemma said gratefully, turning away from the foggy night. "Lots of sugar."

Rebecca raised her eyebrows.

"Hmm, we are in need of something strong tonight," she said playfully. "I think I'll join you."

"What was that all about?" Rebecca waited to ask until the tea was ready and they could sit in comfort. She poured the almost black brew into two waiting mugs.

"She's squatting in the church – with her brother. They're Londoners," Gemma told her. "I let her have some windfalls."

"I never thought of the church as a squat." Rebecca looked serious. "Should we tell the police, d'you think?"

"Oh, no." Gemma was surprised at her positive response and so was Rebecca, who stared at her over the rim of her steaming mug.

"Well, it's not as if they are up to anything—"

"As far as we know," broke in Rebecca.

"You're right, Bec, we don't know. Nor do we know what it's like to be cold and homeless, do we?"

"What are you so uptight about, Gem? They're perfect strangers."

"I'm not uptight, and just because they're strangers doesn't mean we've got to shop them!" Gemma's voice rose and Rebecca blinked. "Oh! If you can't understand, I can't explain!"

There were tears now in Gemma's eyes. Why do I have so much, so much, cried her thoughts, while others have nothing … And why did I have to lose so very much to get it. Confused and very unhappy, she pushed her tea aside and laid her head on her hands.

11

Three days after the terrible Guy Fawkes' night, November began in earnest. A thick fog, dripping wet, hung like a grey blanket over houses and gardens. Gemma stared out of her window, trying to make out the shapes of the trees. The world was very quiet. All sounds of life were muffled by the heavy mist.

Fog-bound, the watcher waited patiently for the heavy mist to lift. The watcher had patience and all the time in the world. One mistake only made the challenge more fun. The watcher's smile was a little grim.

As she stood there dreamily, Gemma was hoping she had seen the last of the press. Banner headlines shouting from the tabloid newspapers had been frightful.

PLASTIC BAG MURDER IN BEDROOM.
"SCARLET WOMAN" YOUTH FOUND DEAD
... and others much the same.

She looked dismally back over the last three terrible days.

The reporters, who seemed to want to camp on her doorstep, had gone. They hadn't bothered her for a whole day now. But there was still a chance that one of them would pop up from behind somewhere when she went out, trying to waylay her. She hadn't realized what an ordeal all that could be. As the hostess of the party, in the house of the murder, she was the focus of their attention, but her friends suffered from them, too.

Gemma and Rebecca's headteacher treated them with great understanding and made sure the school protected them as much as it was possible. As well as announcing Paul's death in assembly, she sent letters to all the parents – a formidable task.

Those of Gemma's party who wanted to stay away for a few days were allowed to gather their books and work at home, or in the library. The girls had planned to do this and Rebecca volunteered to fetch the work for both of them. She had gone into school that morning feeling rather like someone about to enter a new and frightening place, and not the school where she was normally so at home.

Sam was given time off from his job, at least until after Paul's funeral. The inquest was to be held in two days' time, Thursday, but it was to be a simple affair, dealing solely with identification of the boy.

Paul's funeral was arranged for Saturday afternoon. His class and their teachers were going to be there, and Rebecca was dreading it.

All had not gone well for Michael. He was held at the police station again most of the day before. When Gemma phoned Bay Trees in the evening, Rita told her that Michael was too worried and upset to see or talk to anyone.

"He had such a dreadful time there," she told Gemma. "I'm sure you'll understand."

"What did they do to him?" Gemma asked her anxiously.

"It's that threatening letter. The police got a hand-writing expert in."

"What was in the letter?"

"Oh... I don't know ... something like, 'Keep looking over your shoulder, rat. I'm setting a trap for you.' It was signed RIP."

Gemma gave a deep sigh. "Did the expert come to any conclusion?"

"Every other word was printed in a left-handed sort of way and the other words were cut out from a magazine. They said the printing was Michael's, I don't know how they could possibly tell. But that wasn't all, they searched our house yesterday, too."

"Oh no, Rita, how ghastly!" Gemma was horrified at the thought of her neat home being rifled through by strangers.

"What was worse, they found the cut-up magazine

in Michael's room. He hadn't even tried to hide it." Rita went on miserably, "He admitted he'd written it, and said he was afraid to say so before. He said it was a joke."

"Joke?"

"Yes, they were playing a game, apparently, to see who could scare the other most."

Gemma was silent. She had never heard of such a game. Michael would have shared it with her, he shared everything.

"Gemma?" Rita's voice came over the phone anxiously.

"Look," Gemma tried to sound positive, "he might have written that note, and it might have been a game, but that still isn't a motive, or has Michael told them what the so-called secret of Lucy's is?"

"Oh no. He says it isn't true, she made it up."

"There now. We've all got to believe him. We know he isn't a killer, don't we? We have to show him we believe in him."

"Yes, of course, you're right Gemma… He's coming downstairs, bye now." Rita replaced her handset hurriedly.

Oh, Michael! Gemma put her phone down with an aching heart. What a mess!

There was a tap at her door, Gemma called "Come in," and Mrs Jenkins entered. She held a large handbag in her hand. Gemma recognized it. "Angela's" crocodile bag, the one Paul had brought with him as a prop.

"I found this jammed under the big sofa in the drawing-room. Quite a squeeze it was, there's not a lot of space under there. D'you know whose it is? I don't recognize it."

Gemma stared at the bag remembering the way Paul had entered the sitting-room with it over his arm. She suspected then it belonged to his mother. How she had laughed and laughed at him . It seemed an age ago.

"Gemma?" Mrs Jenkins prompted her.

"Oh … yes, it's one of my friends', Mrs J. I'll give it back, they probably left it here by mistake." She spoke calmly, but her hand shook a little as she took it.

"Hmm." Mrs Jenkins sounded smug. "So much for police efficiency! I thought you said they'd combed the place." She tossed her head with satisfaction and left.

Gemma gripped the bag to her chest, trying to calm the hard beating of her heart. Why on earth is it having this effect on me? she wondered. It was just part of Paul's costume. He must have dropped it and forgotten about it in the heat of the moment. But it was unlike Paul to "forget" any of his props. Would she have to give it to the police?

She took the handbag over to her desk and put it down. As she lifted her head, she saw a movement in the foggy garden below. Jet materialized like a shadow from the vague shapes of trees, and stepped on to the lawn near the house. She was carrying the empty plastic bag.

Gemma, with her heart still beating quickly, went down to meet her, curious to know what she wanted.

Dampness had made Jet's spikes of hair stick to her forehead, and her thin jacket was decidedly limp and wet. She looked more waif-like than ever. Gemma resisted the urge to ask her in.

"Ta," Jet said, "for the apples." She did not seem quite so in control that morning.

"Oh," Gemma said quickly. "Take what you want. Take some of the plums too, if there are any left."

"Oh, right, ta," Jet said again. She stood in the back hall, making no move to go.

Her face was pale in the grey morning light, and her nose looked red and pinched. Gemma's conscience pricked her. How could she be so ungenerous?

"Cup of coffee?" Gemma found herself saying.

Seated in the kitchen, Jet seized the hot mugful with her hands, breathing in the steam. She put her elbows on Gemma's table and looked at her.

"You always drink that stuff?" She nodded at Gemma's mug of chocolate.

"It's great, you should try it." Gemma took a rich, warm mouthful.

"Ugh, not me!" Jet shuddered.

An awkward silence fell. Jet studied the kitchen.

"This all yours then?" she asked.

"Umm," said Gemma, trying not to commit herself. Then, to get Jet off that track, "Where's your brother now?"

"Around," Jet said noncommittally. "Seeing some people."

"Friends from London?" Gemma was trying to get Jet to open up a bit more.

"Look," she replied to Gemma's question, "we lived with Mum and she died, right? Then Roach got into a spot of bother on account of he don't always think straight, and me mate said come up 'ere. So we did."

"And someone has promised you a place?" Gemma pressed Jet a little further.

"Yeah," was all the reply she got from her. Jet was gazing abstractedly into nothing, a slight frown creasing her forehead.

A damp and musty smell rose from Jet's clothes as they began to dry. Gemma felt a surge of sympathy for her. She knew what losing a mum was like, and her brother must be difficult to cope with. She wanted to ask her what "bit of bother" Roach had got into, but didn't quite dare.

"What about this murder then?" Jet broke her mood, leaned back in her chair and cocked an eyebrow.

Gemma, taken aback by the sudden question, was firm. "Sorry," she said, "I don't want to talk about it, OK?"

"Suit yourself," Jet shrugged and drained her mug.

"I can let you have some more blankets, if you like. It's so cold at night now," Gemma said impulsively, hoping to make amends for sounding a bit abrupt.

"Yeah, great." Jet stood up.

"Stay put. I'll get them." Gemma left the kitchen. She didn't want Jet following her upstairs.

When she came down again, struggling through the door with four large blankets, she found Jet looking in the kitchen cupboards. She didn't seem in the least put out to be caught doing so. Gemma mentally raised her eyebrows, and then felt guilty because the cupboards were so well-stocked.

She was glad to be able to pass the blankets on. Since duvet covers were bought for all the beds, blankets had taken a back seat and there were masses left in the linen cupboard. Impulsively, Gemma took the rest of their loaf of bread out of the bin and wrapped one of the blankets round it.

"You'll need a hand; I'll carry some," she told Jet.

As they trailed down to the bottom of the garden, she asked, "How'll we get these over the wall?"

"Roach and me got the door open," said Jet.

"Door?"

Gemma realized what she meant when she arrived at the wall. The old door between the churchyard and the Rectory that had stood shut for so long had been levered open. One of its hinges was rusted through and had fallen apart, and some planks were rotten. But when the ivy and nettles had been removed and a bit of pressure put on it, it had opened a little way. Far enough for someone to get through.

Gemma was silent, a small shock of alarm went through her. She felt she was being encroached upon and it made her feel vulnerable. She would have to put an end to that. After they carried the blankets into the church, she'd say something.

Getting into the church was surprisingly easy. The side door to the vestry was small with a slight point to its arch. No one had bothered to board it up. Gemma saw the old lock had been skilfully removed, cleaned a little, oiled, and replaced. Using the blade of a knife, Jet levered the bolt back easily and opened it. No sign of damage could be seen from the outside. Gemma wondered again how many people had used that door.

They stood in the old Victorian vestry, which smelled of dust and cats, trying to adjust their eyes to the dim light. The foggy beams from outside hardly penetrated the dirty glass panes.

Gemma sniffed. Candles, of course. They'd use candles to see by. One or two small stubs were here and there, stuck on chipped saucers. They stood on the window ledges and on the floor beside the two folded sleeping bags. There were a couple of broken chairs, but nothing much else. A holdall and a duffel bag, sundry plastic bags from shops, and a small pile of Gemma's windfalls. It was sparse to the point of empty, but surprisingly neat.

"Welcome to our luxury pad!" Jet mocked as she flung the blankets she was carrying on top of the sleeping bags. Gemma did the same with hers.

Now she was actually standing in the squat and looking at the meagre possessions of the two Londoners, she knew it was going to be hard to tell Jet she didn't want her coming into her garden through the old door. It seemed so mean. Especially if they wanted to pick up windfalls and plums to eat. Better they did that than risk a fall climbing over the wall, for it was unstable, and they would climb it, she knew. Her father had meant to get it rebuilt in the spring.

Perhaps, she thought, I could even help her… Here her thoughts stopped abruptly. Jet may not take easily to being offered help from her.

"Do you miss London?" Gemma found herself asking. She really did want to know more about her.

Jet straightened up from putting the loaf of bread in one of the plastic bags. She smiled her rather appealing grin at Gemma.

"We bin there all our life," she said simply. "What d'you think?"

Gemma felt rebuked.

"Listen," Jet said more kindly, guessing Gemma's curiosity. "You've been kind, OK? You don't want to know why Roach and me had to go. It's not your world, not your scene at all, so give it up."

Then she turned towards Gemma and took a step closer.

"Listen, Gemma. You haven't seen us, right?" There was urgency in her voice. "We're not here, right? If you tell anyone Roach'll get into a lot of trouble. He's OK, Roach, but he needs looking after. He misses Mum. She thought the sun shone for him. So, keep quiet. Cross your heart." This was a long speech for Jet, and her final appeal, redolent of childhood, touched Gemma.

"I won't tell anyone," she said.

"You tell that chum you live with, too. This church is empty – we don't exist. We'll be gone soon, couple a days anyway." Her dark eyes bored into Gemma's blue ones, holding them with an intensity that bordered on desperation. Then her set face relaxed. "You done us a favour with all this." She gestured towards the blankets. "Perhaps Roach and me'll do one for you. We'll just keep an eye on your house, an' if we see anything we think you ought to know about … well, good neighbours, right?"

Gemma didn't know whether to be pleased or worried by Jet's offer of friendship. It seemed all right when it was on her own terms. But the thought of two unknown squatters keeping "an eye" on her home was not entirely reassuring.

"OK, I'm off now," she said, keeping her voice neutral. "Shut the garden door behind me properly. I don't want it used. Besides, it'll look like someone's here, it's been shut for years."

Without looking at Jet again, she left.

Rebecca was waiting when she got home.

"What happened to you? Who's your friend?" She was surveying the two empty mugs on the kitchen table.

Gemma told her.

"Leave it alone, Gem. Don't get drawn in any further. You've done quite enough." Rebecca didn't like the feel of the squatters.

"You didn't see how cold she was, Becca," Gemma tried to explain. "I couldn't just send her off. She came here to thank me for the apples."

"Hum." Rebecca compressed her lips.

"Well, I couldn't just send her away. Perhaps you could." Gemma was getting defiant because she didn't feel easy about it either.

Rebecca didn't want to let it go, but she didn't want to upset Gemma again either.

"I really think we should tell someone about them, Gem," she said gently.

"I promised I wouldn't, Becca. You mustn't either, I said you wouldn't."

Impulsively, Rebecca burst out, "Oh, for goodness' sake, Gemma, use your head. How do you know they aren't into drugs or anything? You don't know what you're letting yourself in for. They probably have a very good reason for lying low. No one would squat in that derelict church if they hadn't." Then, noticing the distress on her friend's face, she said much more lightly, "Next thing we know the place will be crawling with the Mafia, or something!"

Gemma laughed at her friend's description. Rebecca always went far over the top.

"There are just two shivering teenagers in there, that's all, Becca, don't be daft! Look, we'll make a pact, I'll only meet Jet again if you are there to keep me on the straight, how's that?"

"Done!" Rebecca pushed a pile of books towards her.

"With Mr Harding's love," she told Gemma. "Two essays to be in by Friday."

Gemma groaned. "That man has no heart," she sighed as she picked up the books.

"Meet you at lunch," she said and stopped. "By the way, Mrs J found Paul's handbag under the sofa."

Rebecca turned her mouth down. "Angela's handbag, you mean. How on earth did it get there?"

"Search me," Gemma replied. "I guess I should give it to the police. I bet it's his mother's."

The girls raised their shoulders together in a joint shrug.

"Till later," Gemma said and left.

12

Sam, Tracy, Lucy and Guy came over for the evening. It was the first time the Moss sisters and Guy had returned to the Old Rectory since Paul's death, and they had to brace themselves to go back to the place where such a dreadful thing happened. Sam dropped in for supper with Gemma and Rebecca after his work most nights.

They were quiet and subdued when they first arrived and settled in the drawing-room. No one was talking about Paul's funeral, though it was in everyone's mind.

In the corner of the drawing-room the television was on, telling anyone who was interested about the weather, but no one was watching.

Sam said into a little silence, "I wonder how Michael's doing."

No one replied. What could they say? The idea of Michael being thought of as Paul's murderer was appalling and unreal. They knew he wasn't going to join them. Rita said he wouldn't leave the house.

Gemma leaned forward in her chair.

"Come on," she said intensely. "Let's think. We all know Michael and Paul well. Rather, I know Michael very well and we thought we knew Paul, but I'm not so sure now. However, if someone was going to kill Paul, we are in the best position to be aware of possibilities, aren't we?"

Lucy said, with a hint of malice and knowing she was on dangerous ground, "Who would have guessed Michael was going to be chief suspect in a murder? Would you, Gemma?"

Rebecca cut across, shielding Gemma automatically.

"Meaning that even if the so-called secret that you said Paul knew about him was true, then he must also be a killer? Don't be absurd, Lucy. I wonder Gemma lets you in here, seeing it was you who told the police about her cousin."

Gemma sat back in her chair and drew her legs up, tucking them beneath her. It was true, she was having a struggle with herself to continue to see Lucy. She had to tell herself over and over that Lucy had really liked Paul and she had found his body. She reflected too that if Inspector Beale had been questioning her and she had known a secret about Michael, she might have told him, just like Lucy.

It was typical of Rebecca to understand this and defend her. She sipped her chocolate, said nothing, and watched Lucy's face.

Lucy put her coffee down on the floor. She squared up to Rebecca.

"It would seem," her voice rising as she said slowly, "that I am the only one here who really cared about Paul. You knew how he felt about you, Rebecca; you didn't give a toss about him, any of you."

"Your precious Paul," Guy burst out, unable to listen to any more. "Your sainted Paul was a creep!" He didn't care any more if others knew his opinion of Paul, he just hated to hear Lucy standing up for him.

Tracy flinched. Paul was dead. He shouldn't be spoken about like that.

"Stop it!" she said. "This isn't helping anything. This is only making us quarrel."

But Lucy, eyes bright with hidden knowledge, was still furious with Rebecca.

"You can talk, Rebecca Peel. You should be grateful to me. I could have told everyone a thing or two about you, too, but I didn't. You owe me one."

Gemma watched her friend's face freeze. "That's enough, Lucy!" she said. "Stop right there."

Tracy stood up. "Come on, Luce, we're going home."

"Not until I'm good and ready." Lucy kept her seat.

Sam rose. He walked to the door and held it open.

Gemma spoke. "Get out, Lucy," she said coldly.

Looking at each of their faces, shut against her, Lucy got up. She swallowed as tears of rage and hurt filled her eyes. Tracy took her arm and pulled her reluctant figure to the door.

"Look," she said to the others, "she's so unhappy. You know how much she thought of Paul. Come on, let's go, Luce."

"Wait, I'll come, too," Guy said, thinking that he could show his loyalty to Lucy. "Lucy, Tracy, wait for me."

He followed them from the room.

Rebecca's face had gone dead white at first, but was a flaming scarlet now.

"OK, OK," she said, before anyone else could speak. "Lucy's right, little toad! Oh, tell her, Sam."

She buried her hot face in her hands.

"Gem," Sam began. Blast everything, he thought as he looked at Gemma's still face. Why do we have to bring all this up now? Gemma doesn't need this. Impulsively he longed to take her away somewhere, a hide-out, where they would be safe and calm until all the unpleasantness was over. He couldn't, though; where could he find the money? He'd never ask Gemma for it. Sighing inwardly, Sam took a breath.

"Gem, last summer, during the school play, Rebecca and Paul and the other members of the cast spent a lot time together, remember?"

Gemma thought back. She did remember. Rebecca had been drawn into the circle of the "dramatic" group who were in the play with her and

Paul. They were a flamboyant crowd, full of affection; they liked to think they were living in the fast lane. As far as Gemma could see this meant getting low grades due to late-night parties, cutting classes when they thought they could get away with it, and generally going about with an air of sophisticated dissipation.

Gemma had been a bit hurt then. Rebecca seemed to want to be with them more than with her, and she had missed her.

Sam went on.

"After one party at the end of the production, Bec was getting rather tiddly and someone put something in her drink. She doesn't know who."

Rebecca gave a groan.

"Then she said she felt very 'odd and floaty' and the next thing she knew she was doing a striptease on somebody's coffee table! Lucy was at the party and finally managed to get Bec dressed and away, and saw her home.

"Mum and Dad sat us down and gave us both a long lecture the next morning. As if we didn't know about drugs – but I guess they were worried. Bec hadn't taken it on purpose and it could have been a lot worse."

"You never told me, Becca," Gemma said a little sadly.

"Couldn't tell anyone. You see, I don't really know how far I went that night. Lucy won't, or can't, tell me. It's so embarrassing! I just wanted to forget the whole squalid thing. I ask you — a striptease! Anyway, most of the others at the party have left the school now, and Lucy swore blind she wouldn't tell anyone else."

"So, she told Paul? Why?"

"For some reason he wasn't at the party and Lucy wanted to keep in with Paul," Sam explained. "To make him like her. You know how much he loved secrets and this was one to do with Becca. What Lucy was too daft to realize was that instead of blackening her rival in Paul's eyes she was doing just the opposite."

"Before your birthday, Gem," Rebecca took over, "Paul told me he knew about my stripping episode. He said Lucy had told him *everything*. He thought, wrongly, that a shared secret about something as outrageous as that would be something we could giggle over together, you know what he was like. He actually thought we could repeat a version of it in a sort of cabaret!"

"Yes," said Sam ferociously, "Guy's right, he was a creep!"

"And when I told him otherwise, he said he'd spread it around, all the juicy details, some true and some his own invention. I was going to give him his marching orders after the party."

"Only someone else got there first," Sam said flatly.

Well, this doesn't get us anywhere really, Gemma thought. I can no more think of either of these two friends of mine as killers, than I can think of Mike being one. Paul was a toad of the first order. It seems that few of us really knew him. Guy, Sam, Becca and Michael all had reasons to thoroughly dislike him, but … surely, not badly enough to kill him?

"Oh, let's get another drink," Gemma said aloud. "Coffee, you two? I could murder another chocolate." She deliberately said 'murder' to try to shake away the taboo on the word. It didn't work, the word hung in the air like a sharp sword.

"Then I'll go home," said Sam. "We don't have to go to the inquest tomorrow, do we?"

They moved into the kitchen.

Gemma remarked," I thought I had more chocolate than this. Chalk it up on the board as a must, Becca." She gave an enormous yawn and rubbed at her eyes.

"I forgot," Sam said, "Mum says, come over for a meal whenever, and if Rita's off early enough, she's welcome too."

"Great. I could just do with some of Mum's pasta." Becca was feeling a little better now that Gemma knew about her secret escapade. She wondered why she had kept it from her at all.

Gemma's hands holding the milk bottle slipped and she just managed to save it before it fell. A little cry escaped her.

"You OK, Gem?" Rebecca took it from her and put it away. Turning round, she looked into Gemma's face. It was very pale, the dark shadows beneath her eyes looked like bruises against the whiteness of her skin.

"I … just feel so tired and –" she hunted for the word, she felt completely drained of all emotion – "depressed." She sipped the hot chocolate. "I'll take my drink up with me." As she got to the kitchen door she paused and turned to look at her two friends.

"Michael may have had a motive for hating Paul, but he didn't kill him. I don't know who did, but it wasn't Michael."

She went on up the stairs, carrying her mug carefully.

Sam and Rebecca watched her go in silence. Gemma looked so very small and lost. Then they looked at each other, but their eyes slid apart. Neither of them really knew what to think about Michael.

"She's had enough," said Sam helplessly, turning away from the question of Michael's guilt or innocence. It was too tough a subject.

On Gemma's desk the handbag lay forgotten, like an unexploded bomb.

Gemma's head felt very heavy. She tried to go over the events of the evening, but her thoughts kept getting jumbled up however much she tried to put them in order. The cosy world of friendships that helped to support her through the weeks before the murder had blown apart, and she felt miserable.

Fancy Becca keeping that from me, she thought

sadly, as she got ready for bed, well … well … but her thoughts drifted away. She only knew that for the first time since her parents died, she felt terribly, terribly lonely.

Tired tears threatened to roll down her cheeks, but she rubbed her eyes hard. Not tonight, she told herself.

Everything would just have to wait until the morning. She'd sort it all out then.

How sleepy she felt. More tired than she had ever been. Sleep seemed to be imperative.

I'll have a shower in the morning, was her last conscious thought as she fell into bed and was asleep without turning off the light.

13

"Sam!" Rebecca sounded frantic. She was clutching the telephone so hard her knuckles were white.

"Hold on, Bec, where's the fire?" He held the receiver away from his ear.

"I can't wake Gemma. She won't budge. Should I get a doctor? Where's Mum?"

"The poor girl's tired out, she doesn't want you jumping up and down on her."

"Sam, this is serious. I'm terrified!"

"OK, OK." Sam got the message. "Mum's just left. I could try to reach her on the mobile. She'll be in some traffic jam by now, I expect."

"Please, Sam. I really don't like the look of Gemma."

"Done," Sam said crisply. "Hold on, Bec," he said again, "I'm on my way."

Sam was right, Dr Peel was in a traffic jam when she answered his call on her mobile phone. With the promise of her immediate appearance he sprinted over to the Old Rectory. Rebecca let him in and took him upstairs. Brother and sister stood by Gemma's bedside, looking down at her still figure.

"Mum says to get her on her feet and try to keep her awake until she gets here. Try waking her, Bec."

Rebecca leaned over Gemma and called her name loudly. Gemma didn't respond. She looked very peaceful with her fair, short hair spreading like a little halo on the pillow, and her breathing coming deep and even.

"Gemma, wake up!" Rebecca began to shake her.

Sam felt panic rising. Gemma had to wake up, she had to...

He leaned over and began to slap Gemma's face gently on each cheek. After about the tenth time her eyelids flickered.

"Let's lift her up."

Rebecca put her arms round Gemma's shoulders and began to pull, while Sam took both her elbows, tugging on them to raise her up to a sitting position. Gemma's head rolled forward, but she feebly tried to right it. It flopped again.

"On her feet," commanded Sam. He pulled back the bedclothes and lifted Gemma's pyjama-clad legs sideways so that her feet touched the floor.

"Ready? One, two, three..." They lifted her upright between them, taking her full weight. Gemma's body sagged at the knees and her head leaned on Sam's shoulder. He felt her soft hair brush his cheek and a rush of tenderness for the sleeping girl filled him.

"Come on, Gem, come on girl, walk … walk … walk…" he urged her. They dragged her up and down the room.

By degrees Gemma's weight began to shift from her friends' support to her own legs. Her heavy head wavered on her neck, but didn't fall forward any more, just nodded in a drunken way.

"Black coffee!" Sam commanded Rebecca. "Forget her chocolate, she needs caffeine. I'll keep her going."

By the time Rebecca returned with the black brew, as strong as she could make it, Gemma was sitting on her bed, supported by Sam but conscious.

Her blue eyes were vague and unfocused, but she was in charge of herself again. She held out a shaky hand to Rebecca and grasped at her sleeve feebly.

Rebecca sat on her other side; Sam didn't look as if he was going to give up the bit of her he was in charge of. She held the mug to Gemma's lips.

"No talking, Gem, just drinking," she said, her own green eyes filling with relieved tears.

Gemma sipped and coughed.

The door bell rang.

"Mum!" Sam ran down to let her in. Rebecca's relief on seeing her mother enter Gemma's room was boundless. Her familiar figure brought with it safety and comfort. She hadn't realized quite how frightened she had been.

They propped Gemma up in her bed now that she was fully awake. Dr Peel examined her and pronounced that she would be fine just as soon as the drug, which it must have been, had worked its way through her system. She was to take it easy, but there should be no ill effects.

"Which sleeping pills did you take, Gemma?" she asked, eyeing the empty mug beside the bed. "Did your doctor give you any to help you when you couldn't sleep?"

"I do have some," Gemma said, "but last night I didn't take any. I just suddenly felt very sleepy."

"Had you had anything to eat or drink before turning in?"

"Only chocolate. I always have that."

Dr Peel looked puzzled. "Well, you could just be sleeping off the effects of too many shocks, the body can do things like that if it has to, you know. But you seemed drugged to me. Perhaps you should go into hospital for observation."

"Oh, no!" Gemma was startled. She wasn't sick.

Dr Peel smiled at her alarmed expression.

"Well, promise me you'll get in touch if you feel odd or anything at all, won't you?"

Gemma promised.

Outside the door Dr Peel said, "Rebecca, in confidence, has Gemma been very depressed?"

Rebecca considered. Gemma was always a quiet

sort of person, and naturally her parents' death's had shaken her terribly. Sad she had been, but not depressed; that is, not until last night.

"She was a bit low when she went to bed," she said truthfully.

"Hmm. You don't think she might have felt … well, felt … she'd had enough?" Dr Peel spoke tactfully.

"Enough?" Rebecca gasped, suddenly understanding what her mother was implying.

"Where does she keep the sleeping pills?"

Rebecca led her mother to the bathroom and opened the medicine cabinet. She reached for a small brown bottle and held it out.

Dr Peel tipped the white tablets on to her palm. The bottle had held thirty and there were only ten left. There was no way of knowing when they had been taken. She sighed.

Downstairs she looked at her worried son and daughter. "Just keep an eye on Gemma, won't you?" she directed them. "Bring her home with us if you think she needs it. Sam, I think you'd better stay here, too, at least until after the weekend, just to give Becca a little backup."

She flashed a rallying smile at them both, and went.

14

Gemma got up and dressed later in the morning, but work was out of the question. Her head swam when she tried to concentrate and she had an enormous thirst.

"Why on earth did I sleep so deeply?" Gemma wondered aloud for the hundredth time. Thinking about it was hard enough. Her thoughts rolled around in her head like marbles. She sat with Rebecca and Sam in the kitchen. It was so good to have Sam with them for a night or two. She would have liked to have stretched out her small hand to cover his larger one as it lay upon the kitchen table. She looked at his serious profile and brown, wavy, unruly hair and longed to let him know just how she felt about him.

But since her birthday night he had seemed more

distant. It was hard to say how; he was as supportive as ever but that special smile that crinkled the corner of his eyes, the one she knew was for her alone, had gone. Was it something she had done? Or was the whole messy business making him clam up inside. Would she have to wait until everything was settled and over before she would see that smile again?

"Are you sure you didn't take any pills last night?" Rebecca asked, breaking into her thoughts.

Gemma started.

"I know I was dead tired … and very miserable. But I didn't take a pill," she replied. "I had no need, I was asleep on my feet."

Rebecca couldn't concentrate on school work either. She, too, kept returning to the mystery of Gemma's drugged sleep. She was sure that was what it was. Gemma had taken a gulp or two of her chocolate in the kitchen before she went up, but had begun to feel woozy shortly before. Perhaps that was why she nearly dropped the milk bottle. On the other hand, it could have been genuine tiredness. But Gemma had drunk two cups of chocolate.

Before Gemma joined them, Rebecca had talked it over with Sam. He suggested they look for the chocolate tin, the one that Gemma said was nearly empty. They found it in the waste bin, where Gemma must have put it last night after she had scraped the last spoonful. The few grains of choco-late powder clinging to the sides of the tin looked harmless enough. Sam didn't think there was anything sinister about it, but all the same, Rebecca put it away on a shelf in the utility room. Just in case, she thought.

They didn't mention any of this to Gemma. There were more pressing things to ponder over. The inquest on Paul's death was taking place the next day, and their thoughts often went out to Michael, who was still under suspicion.

Also, the quarrel with Lucy had left a nasty taste in their mouths. It was doubtful if they could ever feel the same friendship towards Lucy again, but they also felt depleted without their small group of friends. What was to be done?

Silently, however, the poisonous drip of suspicion leaked into all their minds unbidden. Someone had hit Paul over the head with the heavy lamp – and then stuffed his unconscious head into a plastic bag to finish him off. As far as they knew there was no one else in the house but themselves to do it.

If Michael hadn't done it, then who?

For the millionth time Gemma ticked everyone off.

Sam was stuck in the cellar. Michael would have seen him if he had left it.

Rebecca, in the games-room, could have slipped up the back stairs, unseen, done the deed and returned. But Paul's pathetic attempt to blackmail her didn't seem to give her enough cause.

Lucy, in the attic, had found the body and wouldn't have wanted Paul dead anyway.

Tracy, in the kitchen, had no quarrel with Paul as far as she knew.

Guy, in the bathroom on the first-floor landing, didn't like Paul for being the sort of boy he was and hated him for being his rival for Lucy's admiration. He had the best opportunity, and strength, but was his motive strong enough to make him kill? Gemma doubted it.

Michael had been stationed in the drawing-room which had easy access to any part of the house while they were all in their rooms. He could have planned to go up in the dark, taking the plastic fruit as cover, seized the lamp, hit an unsuspecting Paul, put on the bag and tied it, and then wiped all traces off with his large handkerchief, leaving Paul to die of suffocation. There would still be time to return to his post minutes before the alarm went off. But, as his finger-prints were on the lamp, perhaps there hadn't been time to do that last thing.

He would have had to prepare for it, of course, by putting the plastic bag as well as the handkerchief in his pocket. The idea was horrible, cold-blooded. But why? What for? She wouldn't ever believe he was a murderer, no matter what. Not Michael. He was like her brother and she loved him.

Gemma had been sitting in the dining-room. She had heard nothing, seen nothing ... wait a moment ... she'd slipped out for a painkiller.

Michael must have been in the drawing-room then, but he could have done the murder by that time; it was nearly at the end of the ten minutes and she'd had to make a dash. Was the drawing-room door open when she returned? If so, he must have still been upstairs. It was so dark and the fireworks were going off all the time, but it was impossible to know for sure.

She hadn't told the police when they asked about her movements and anyway she hadn't seen anything suspicious. There was no one on the landing or in the passage as far as she knew. Michael had been returning Paul's plastic fruit to him sometime then. Perhaps he had seen her flash past him on the landing. She hadn't been aware of him and it didn't really add much to the mystery.

Gemma sighed. Those minutes in the darkened dining-room had been her last moments of comparative peace of mind.

The phone rang and she let Rebecca or Sam answer it. Feeling very lazy, she was curled up on the sofa with a rug over her knees even though the fire was lit. Rebecca had been pampering her, and had made her some hot lemon water to sip.

"That was Tracy," Rebecca reported, coming in. "She says how about meeting at The Figaro later for a pizza. Lucy won't be there but Tracy says she and Guy would like it if we came. They feel awkward about the other night."

"What did you say?" asked Gemma.

"I said I'd phone back when I'd seen how you are. Just said you'd felt a bit groggy today."

Gemma was undecided. "What does Sam think?" she asked, passing the buck.

"Actually, Sam thinks it may be a good step, seeing as the offer is coming from them. They seem eager for contact." Gemma still hesitated.

"Well, look," Rebecca said, understanding her feelings, "suppose Sam and I go. We can say you're resting, which is true, and we won't be late."

"Fine." Relief showed on Gemma's face and Rebecca grinned.

"All in aid of keeping the troops' morale up. Sure you won't mind about being here on your own?"

"Go," said Gemma. "It'll probably do me good to be quiet. I'll be OK."

Sam and Rebecca went out about six-thirty. Gemma hadn't been alone for an evening since her return to the Old Rectory; it would be in the nature of an experiment, she told herself. She armed herself with a book and returned to the fire. There was a film on the box she wanted to see later. It might, she thought, be quite good to be lazy and please herself.

But it wasn't. Gemma soon tossed her book aside and turned on the television, but the programmes didn't hold her attention either. She became all too aware of the large empty house around her and the November night outside the windows.

It was blowing a gale and the trees in the garden were sighing and rustling. Their boughs creaked as the strong wind tugged at them. Some of the old beams of the house were creaking as well. Sometimes,

Gemma shivered, it sounded like footsteps coming down the stairs.

She got up and turned on another lamp. Lit with only one light, the drawing-room held too many shadows in the corners.

There were always moans in the chimney when the wind came from a certain quarter. In the past, when Gemma and her parents had sat round the fire, she thought the sound it made was kind and friendly, like an enormous hum. Tonight it just sounded weird and somehow threatening. It rose and fell like a ghostly lost soul.

Then, amongst the creaks and rattles of the old windows and the general noise of the gale, she heard tapping. It was rhythmic and insistent, and didn't end when the gusts of wind died down to take a breath before starting again. There was something urgent about it.

Gemma's scalp began to creep.

The noise wouldn't go away. Tap, tap, tap. She simply had to go and see what it was, it was driving her crazy.

Getting slowly to her feet, she opened the drawing-room door on to the inky, unlit hall. She groped for the switch. Flooding it with electric light helped a bit, but it was pitch black in the passage and the rooms beyond the baize door, too, and now the tapping sounded much louder.

Someone, she realized, was knocking on the back door.

Jet?

Turning on every light she could, Gemma finally got to the door. Half of it was made of panes of glass and now she could see there was a figure close up against it. It couldn't be Jet. It was the shape of a man banging on the wooden part of the door with his knuckles. She reached the switch for the outside light and turned it on him like a spotlight.

The tapping ceased abruptly and Gemma saw a face pressing hard against the glass, flattened and distorted. Whoever it was was trying to get a look at her.

Gemma shouted through the door, "What d'you want?"

"Wha?" came the reply faintly through the noise outside.

"I said, what do you want?" Gemma called out, louder and more distinctly.

"I got a message," the unknown man shouted back. "For Gemma."

"Who from?"

The face outside mouthed something that she didn't catch.

Gemma thought, this is silly, standing here both sides of this door shouting at each other.

"Just a minute," she called. "I'll open the door."

She withdrew the bolt and turned the stiff old key with difficulty. The door practically flew open with the force of the wind behind it, and the unknown messenger got propelled into the house at the same time.

"Are you Roach?" Gemma said as inspiration struck her. "Help me get this door shut." She was struggling, battling to shut it again against the force of the wind.

"Yeah, how'd you guess?" Roach leaned his thin body against the door and together they managed to get it closed. They stood back, panting slightly, and stared at each other.

He wasn't a mature man, Gemma realized, but he looked older than Jet. She had imagined him the younger brother but he was about Sam's age, she reckoned. He was built like a steel wire, stronger than his looks led you to believe, and about as tall as Rebecca. His brown hair had been swept away from his face by the wind. It was shoulder-length, and it revealed a ferrety sort of face, long nose, thin mouth and not much chin.

Gemma said, "So, Jet sent you."

"Yeah," Roach said again.

"Go on, then," she prompted him. "You have a message from Jet?" He seemed to have dried up.

"Yeah, well. She says to come over tomorrow."

Gemma gave a short sigh of impatience.

"Come over where? And if she wanted to see me, why hasn't she come herself?"

Communication was obviously not one of Roach's best subjects. He took it bit by bit.

"Come over to the squat," he said with care. "She's done her ankle."

"Done her ankle? How?"

"Over the wall."

"She was climbing the wall?" Gemma felt the need to clarify every statement Roach said.

A twinge of guilt dug at her. She had stopped Jet using the old garden door and now she had got hurt climbing the wall that Gemma had known was dodgy.

"Did you climb over the wall, too?"

Roach gave a snort. "Nah, not me. That's stupid, I come by the door."

Gemma thought, he's not as daft as he looks.

"Poor Jet," she said aloud. "I'm so sorry. I'll come now." She suddenly remembered her promise to Rebecca, but Jet was hurt so that had to be different.

"Nah," said Roach. "It's late tonight."

"I could call a doctor … or, you could bring her in here," Gemma found herself offering.

"Nah, she wouldn't like that."

"Well, let me come to her. I've got stuff to put on her ankle, and bandages. Wait and I'll get them."

Roach stepped quickly between her and the door to the hall.

"Nah," he said again, earnestness making his voice louder. "You give me the stuff. She's tired now – prob'ly asleep." Then he added, as if a new thought struck him, "She knows something, she says to say, but says it'll keep, she's *seen* something. Come tomorrow, in the day. She'll be OK tonight."

Anxiety gripped Gemma. She was intrigued and worried. Jet didn't seem the sort of person to mess about. This had to be important. Jet had found something out. Something about Paul's murder? She had said she would watch the place.

"Roach," she asked him, "d'you know what it's about?"

"Search me," Roach replied with a shrug of his thin shoulders. Then he added, "If Jet says you'll want to know, you will, that's all."

He straightened up.

"Right, I'm off."

"Wait a second. I haven't got the bandages yet; I've also got some rolls and ham. Hang on and I'll get it all." Gemma's kind heart couldn't bear to send Roach off to that dismal vestry with nothing to eat.

"Oh, ta," he said, taking the plastic bag full of first aid stuff, rolls and sliced ham from her. He pulled the door open and once again they battled together to shut it.

Alone again, Gemma realized she was almost disappointed that Jet had not wanted her to go to her. Oh, for goodness' sake, she scolded herself. You don't need Roach's company – or Jet's. I know they say any port in a storm – but there is a limit!

Returning to the warmth of the fire and the gentle drone of the box she felt calmer. She would tell Becca about Roach's visit, and perhaps they would both go to the squat tomorrow. Then Becca would realize that they weren't sinister at all, only two homeless people in an unfamiliar town, one of whom was hurt.

She wondered if she should tell Sam. What would

his reaction to the squatters be? She wanted to confide in him and have his approval for giving them a hand. But would he approve? Sam had become so … not distant exactly, but removed, removed from her. What was it? Had he simply gone off her? Maybe Rebecca knew; should she ask her? Well, she wouldn't risk telling him, and anyway she had promised not to.

She settled down again.

The titles of the film she wanted to watch started to roll, but Gemma's eyes drooped.

I do believe I'm too sleepy to watch this after all. She yawned. As if I've not had enough sleep.

No good, I must go up. The others will understand when they come home.

Glad Sam's here anyway. Her thoughts went on as she mounted the stairs. I wish … I wish I knew what … I wish I knew the way to reach him…

The gale blew itself out, and Gemma slept.

15

Gemma woke early. A wintry dawn had left the sky pale and cloudy. She remembered with a pang of dread that it was the day of the inquest, but was surprised to find she felt fresher than she had for weeks.

Perhaps, she hoped as she dressed, I'll be able to get down to those essays today. Her eyes, straying over to the pile of books on her desk, saw the crocodile handbag. She had completely forgotten it.

Action on that has to be taken today, she thought, and went across to pick it up. She'd ring the police station and they could deal with it.

It was a handsome bag, expensive and shiny. Gemma opened it automatically. There was a small mirror in the side pocket, a tiny change purse and a slender book, just big enough to lie easily inside the richly lined interior.

The book had a red-leather binding and Gemma saw, as she took it out, it was a diary. The year was printed in gold on the front.

"Posh!" Gemma said aloud and opened it. It was Paul's diary. His name and address was written in his flowery hand on the flyleaf. Her sense of propriety checked her for an instant. Private diaries should not be read. But Paul was dead, he couldn't be hurt by what she was doing. Anyway, she thought, it won't be very interesting, it'll be all about himself.

Gemma was wrong.

She opened it at random, at a week during the Easter term.

April 11th. Useful day. Found DM smoking you-know-what down by the big tree. Difficult to prove, but I'll get a few perks from that one. Have my eye on his Omega sweatshirt.

"The slimeball!" Gemma was appalled. That must be Don Maddon. I wondered why Paul was wearing his Omega. She turned more pages, horribly fascinated. There were a few more entries with pathetic little secrets Paul had wormed out of different people, most of them younger than he was.

Then she arrived at the first week in June. After a few days full of great moans about the coming exams, the entry for that Friday leaped out at her, written in large capital letters: *June 5th. GOT HIM. THE BEST OF THE BAG. WRIGGLE, WRIGGLE, MIKE PALMER, YOU'RE CAUGHT!!!*

Gemma slowly sat down at her desk and read on.

They say that fate never takes a hand in the affairs of men, but what else led me to be in the right passage at the right time and see what I saw and who I saw doing it? Don't ask me how he got the key, I'm not a psychic, but there he was stealing a certain exam paper not long before the date of the exam. He must have thought the fates were on his side that day, but guess what – he was wrong!! To watch and to wait will be my game.

"Michael? Does he mean he saw Michael steal the exam paper?" Stunned, Gemma turned the page.

A week later there was the entry about the maths exam; Gemma remembered it well. They had all been nervous about it. Michael the most. He'd got D in his mocks.

Two days later Paul had written,

June 7th. The stupid nutter hasn't a clue. Finding the paper was a doddle. Why didn't he destroy it? I would. Luckily for me he didn't and I've got it, as I've got him, under my boot!

Tucked inside the next page was a folded piece of typewritten paper. It was the A-level maths exam paper for that year. Written in biro between the maths questions were notes on the answers. It was, without doubt, Michael's handwriting.

"Oh God," breathed Gemma. "Michael, what have you done?"

Bleakly, she turned the pages of the little book. There were entries that said things like, *Mikey came up trumps again!* Or *Speak nicely to Mikey, want the new "Spaceballers" video.* Then, standing out like a laser beam, with a receipt for a motorbike helmet stuck to the page, was the entry: *To my bike, from Mike!*

Tears blurred Gemma's eyes. "He was just bleeding him," she breathed aloud.

Two days before the last entry she saw: *November 3rd. Hmmm. Got one of THOSE letters today. Three guesses who sent it! However, dear Diary, you're going to stick close to me from now on. You'll never leave my side. We know he's a schmuck, don't we, but we ain't taking any chances.* Then in brackets, *Yuk! Yuk!*

So that was why Paul had brought the diary with him, it was obvious. Perhaps, wanting to make sure of its safety, he'd squeezed the bag under the sofa himself. No one would open it, they wouldn't know it was there. A quick shove while everyone was looking at their cards was all it needed. He could fish it out any time, or so he thought.

"Filthy pig!" Gemma threw the diary across the room and buried her head in her hands, sobbing hard. When at last her desperate crying stopped and her breathing had ceased its violent spasms, she found she could think clearly again.

OK, now I know what Michael's secret is and I must be the only one who does. Paul didn't tell Lucy, only gave her his name. One thing I am sure about: he may be a cheat, but Michael is no killer.

The urge to rush round to Bay Trees and see him was very strong, but she knew she should speak to him and give him some warning first. She'd ring the station about the bag and then try to reach Michael. Together they would decide what to do with the diary, although her impulse was to destroy it and the exam paper there and then. The police would never hear of it from her lips, but Michael should have a say in what ought to happen to it.

Gemma sat at her desk for some long minutes, thinking of her cousin. What an utter idiot he's been, she thought. She remembered the pressure Michael felt over those exams in the summer. He'd wanted to please Rita so desperately and to do well. And it wasn't only Rita. She knew that her own father had said there would be a position in the family business for Michael, if he proved himself worthy. She knew, too, that Michael thought the sun shone out of his uncle's eyes, he admired him so much. Maths was always his pitfall.

But Michael, to everyone's delight, had passed the exam with flying colours.

Perhaps, Gemma went on musing, that was one of the reasons her father was altering his will. Perhaps Michael had proved himself to be worthy of a place in the firm and would get his reward.

Oh, Dad! she thought miserably. Look at us now!

The phone by her bed rang loudly and made her jump.

It was eight o'clock already and Rita was phoning Gemma from her office. She had gone in early as the inquest was to be held at noon, and she had things to do.

152

She and Gemma had kept in touch by phone each day since the tragedy. But with Rita's schedule of work, some of which she couldn't just drop, and her preoccupation with Michael's predicament, they had not seen each other.

Gemma was glad to hear her aunt's voice. Rita sounded strained and tired, but coping.

"How's Michael?" Gemma asked.

She could hear Rita's deep release of breath and she wondered what she was going to say.

"He's almost in pieces, Gemma. The police keep coming to the house with more questions. They believe he did it, but they haven't got enough evidence yet. They are trying to make him confess."

Gemma heard the tremor in Rita's voice. She said as confidently as she could, "Well, he can't do that, can he? He didn't do it."

"If we could only find out who did."

Gemma tried to rally her aunt. "The funeral's on Saturday. After that things will begin to get more settled, more normal." She tried to sound positive.

Rita said, rather pitifully, "I'd love to see you, Gemma. I'm home today after the inquest."

"I'll come over after lunch when you're back," said Gemma, wishing to comfort her. "We'll talk it all through then." And I might get a word alone with Michael, she added to herself.

Rita seemed cheered by the thought of her visit, and the call ended on a more hopeful note.

"You're right, Gemma dear," she said. "We must

be sensible and take one step at a time."

Gemma replaced the phone and immediately rang Michael. She heard the phone ring for a long time but at last, to her relief, it was lifted and Michael's voice, very shaky, said, "Hello?"

A rush of gladness at hearing him again swamped Gemma. She said, "Michael, it's me, Gemma. How're you doing?" She wouldn't barge at him, she'd come at it gradually.

"OK." His voice was steadier. He must have thought it was the police again. "You?"

"Yeah, fine." She paused, uncertainly. "Listen, Mike, something's come up. We must talk, I've got to see you."

Another pause; Gemma thought she could hear him breathing.

"Michael," she repeated, "we have to talk." No answer.

"Listen, I've found Paul's diary."

Still silence.

"Mike, his *diary*. *I know*." Oh God, make him understand, she prayed. I don't want to have to spell it out.

Still the silence hung between them like a long thick rope.

"Michael, are you there?" Gemma heard the phone at the other end being quietly put back into its cradle.

"Mike!" she shouted in frustration. "Oh damn!"

It was the shock, she thought. He needed time, I'll

try again, and she pressed the buttons. This time the receiver was not lifted. She couldn't just drop everything and rush over; it would be impossible to explain to Sam and Becca without telling lies and she couldn't face doing that to them.

But she was very worried about Michael, he sounded so odd. Worst of all, she hadn't had the time to reassure him, to say she wouldn't tell, he was safe.

Breakfast was a scrappy affair. Sam seemed preoccupied and Rebecca looked at her friend's strained face as she pushed her toast and honey away, not hungry.

"OK?" she asked her.

"Fine." Gemma wanted to blurt out that things were not fine, that Michael was a cheat and in grave danger of being arrested for a murder she was still sure he didn't do, even though the evidence was getting stacked against him. But Becca and Sam, like everyone else, had to remain ignorant about the diary. She hated keeping anything from them. She tried to appear normal.

"I've rung the police about the handbag," she said, trying a safe subject. "They're sending someone over for it this morning. I'll stay around."

All three of them were feeling uneasy and restless.

"How was your pizza?" Gemma asked, trying again.

"Fine," they said together, and laughed.

"It was OK, Gem," Sam said. "We kept things light; Guy and Tracy just wanted to be friendly.

Lucy has been ordered to rest by her doctor apparently, he's given her tranquillizers and their parents are packing her off to a cousin or someone."

"No, not far away," he added, seeing Gemma's eyebrows rise. "PC Plod can reach her, if he needs to."

"Poor Luce," said Gemma.

"Don't waste your sympathy." Rebecca's voice was quite harsh. She had not forgiven Lucy for her treachery.

"We've asked Guy and Tracy back here tonight, OK, Gem?"

"OK," Gemma agreed. She found she didn't care one way or the other. She must talk to Michael, nothing mattered as much as that. I'll go after breakfast, she thought. But what if he doesn't answer the door, have I the right to barge in?

Sam decided to go home and fetch some tapes.

"I'll see you this afternoon," he said as he left.

Suddenly Gemma remembered Roach's visit in the night. The diary business had knocked it out of her head, made it seem unreal somehow. She must tell Rebecca about her proposed visit to Jet that afternoon. She knew Rebecca was not convinced that they should have anything to do with the squatters, she had said so before, but when Gemma said, "Becca, I feel bound by my promise to Roach, and anyway, Jet said she had something important to tell me," Rebecca gave in.

"I'll meet you here when you get back from

Rita's," she reassured her. "We'll face them together, never fear."

Then Rebecca, determined to keep normality going even if it meant studying, took herself off to the library to get lost in some books in the reference section.

Gemma was alone again. Outside the house the world was bright with autumn sunshine. It was sparkling after the gales of the night before. The fierce winds had blown nearly all the remaining leaves off the trees. Now they stood bare with their strong branches and slender twigs making black patterns against a washed blue sky.

Gemma stood at her back door. Feeling the sun on her face after the gloomy days before was like bathing in fizzy lemonade. She needed that.

Very reluctant to go inside, and thinking it may calm her worries, Gemma thrust her hands into the sleeves of her warm jumper and strolled around the orchard.

The fallen apples left lying on the ground and abandoned by the hungry summer wasps squashed under her feet.

Strange, she mused, this place is full of memories of Mum and Dad, I feel closer to them here than anywhere. I can think of them and all the things we did together and it doesn't hurt so much when I'm here. That's why I just can't leave it. Kind house, kind Old Rectory.

She went down to the orchard gate and looked at

it. There were traces of its recent move, but the wooden door had been pulled and shoved back to its place. The wall, however, had lost another stone.

Why had Jet wanted her to come? What had she seen? Gemma would feel a lot easier when they weren't in the church any more. They were not a welcome presence, waifs or not.

But Gemma's thoughts were still with Michael. Nagging anxiety about her cousin followed her, even there. Why had he rung off without speaking to her? What was he thinking?

I'll get rid of the diary myself, she decided. That'll help. That'll make him know he's safe. I'll do it now.

Sunny though the morning was, the air was full of frosty nights to come. It made her shiver and she went back to the house. She left the breakfast washing-up in the sink, and climbed up to her bedroom.

Paul's diary was where she had thrown it, lying against a wall. The exam paper had fluttered loose and was on the floor nearby.

Gemma picked both up. She knew exactly what she was going to do. She also knew she intended to destroy what the police might think was vital evidence of a serious crime. If they found out it would not be pleasant. Tough, she thought. What they don't know won't hurt them, or me.

Back in the kitchen she ripped the cover off the diary and tore the pages and the tell-tale paper into as many tiny pieces as she could. When that was done, she put them in the sink and soaked the pieces thoroughly.

Leaving them for a moment she turned her attention to the red leather cover. This she attacked with the kitchen scissors, cutting where she could. The remains were then thrust into a plastic bag and buried deep in the rubbish bin full of the garbage from breakfast, along with old peel, egg shells and limp tea bags.

Almost done, she gathered up the soggy remains of the bits of paper and swished them into the waste disposal unit, turning it full on. It ground away. When she peered inside, every bit had vanished. The only remaining thing to do was to remove the rubbish bag from the kitchen and bury it deep in the wheely bin outside.

It was done. Nothing of Paul's diary was left to threaten Michael's peace of mind. Gemma felt a deep satisfaction.

Upstairs again, she sat at her desk, but her hands had begun to tremble with the reaction to it all and her mind was in a turmoil. Until she had contacted Michael, there would be no peace for her. She pushed the books aside and sighed.

The phone rang again.

"I've just had a weird call from Michael, Gemma." Rita's voice was tight with control.

Gemma's heart lurched. He mustn't confess now, not now he was safe. Her tongue went stiff.

"He just said ... he just said ... 'Mum'. I think he

was crying. Please, Gemma could you go over? I'm stuck here."

Gemma pulled herself together.

"Right. I'll wait with him till you come. Don't worry, Rita. I'll go now."

After all, that was what she wanted to do. She replaced the phone and stood for a second collecting her thoughts. Then, feeling that speed was imperative, she strode quickly to her door.

It wouldn't open.

Gemma pulled at it, then realized that it had been locked from the outside. She stared at her closed door in amazement and thought she heard quiet footsteps in the passage.

"Becca!" she called. "Sam, are you back?"

There was another little sound like an animal sniffing, or was it a quick chuckle? There was someone – or something – waiting on the other side. Straightening her shoulders, she grabbed the door handle and turned and pulled again. It wouldn't move.

The Old Rectory had large old-fashioned keys in most of its locks. None of the occupants of the house had ever wanted to destroy the charm of the deeply panelled doors and their semi-ornate furnishings which included the keys.

"Who's there?" Gemma felt panic rising. "Is anyone there?"

There was no answer.

"Oh, God!" Gemma whispered. "I don't know what to do."

16

Rebecca was not having a very good morning. She finally arrived at the library at around eleven. The buses were intolerably slow and there were endless traffic jams. On arrival there was another delay in finding the book she needed, which meant she would have to take notes very hastily if she was to get back through the traffic to Gemma by lunch-time.

It was a brainless idea, she thought, scowling at her untidy handwriting. What made me think I could get anything done this morning? She was carefully not admitting to herself it was more the idea of doing something extremely normal, like getting on a bus, that attracted her. She began to feel, as the days after Paul's murder wore on, that she and Gemma were living a life apart from everyone else.

This was, up to a point, true.

She abandoned the library and jogged her way back in the bus, hoping Gemma would have had the good sense to eat her lunch if she was hungry. She was much later than she intended.

Gemma was standing in front of her bedroom door, wringing her hands. Fear had robbed her of all thought and began to make her knees feel weak. She slumped on to her bed.

Someone had locked her in.

Gemma's breath came through her mouth in shallow gasps. Quiet, she told her racing heart, just calm down, I have to think. The image of the dead rat came to her suddenly and made her gasp. That was the very first horror, since then...

Testing her legs she stood up slowly, listening all the time for other alien sounds. None came. She stood there, irresolute, for a long moment.

Then she became aware of a different sound. This time beyond the windows. It was a fresh crackling noise, like fat sizzling in a frying pan.

Gemma, now truly terrified, rushed to her window and after struggling for an agonizing minute with the safety catch, threw up the sash and looked down. On the terrace below her a small bonfire was blazing hungrily. It was close up against the French windows of the drawing-room, out of sight of the back door. An acrid plume of smoke, black and sooty, engulfed her horrified face. Hastily she shut the window and turned back into the room.

Like a trapped animal she ran once more to the door and tugged hard at the knob. The door opened at once and the shock of its sudden movement made Gemma stagger. She was free.

Down the stairs and out around the house she raced, until she was beside the fire. It was built of old newspapers and some fallen twigs. Not a very large blaze, but frighteningly close to the house just the same. Seizing a broom from the back-hall passage she scattered the flaming embers and half-burnt wood, until the fire was no longer a threat.

Panting hard, Gemma surveyed the blackened mess on her terrace. Her knees gave way again and she sat down gratefully on a low wall that divided the terrace from the lawn.

She was sweating and shaking.

The watcher saw it all and smiled.

"Water," Gemma said aloud, her voice was a croak but the sound of it was comforting. "Thirsty."

In the kitchen she took long pulls of a tall glass of water until she was satisfied and gasping. As she looked around it was obvious that nothing in there had been disturbed. She made herself go from room to room. Everything was as it should be.

I must go to Michael, was all she could think.

Acting quickly, Gemma scribbled a note for Rebecca.

Becca, I'm scared. Gone to Rita's. Come there, please. G. She wouldn't mention Michael's name.

She hoped that by the time Becca arrived they'd have talked about the diary and got that well over. Then we can decide what to do about all this; tell the police, or something.

Putting the note on the kitchen table and grabbing her coat, scarf and bag, Gemma left through the back door, her usual route. She had been meaning to get a new set of keys for Rebecca, but it had slipped her mind, so she had held on to the back-door key, and Rebecca had the front.

Gemma arrived at Rita's house agitated and out of breath. She had run a large part of the way. As she pushed open the garden gate and went up the familiar path her heart rate lessened and she felt a little calmer. Bay Trees was so orderly, so neat, and so familiar. She rummaged for the key she still kept in her bag, found it, unlocked the door and went inside.

"Michael!" she shouted. "Michael, it's me, Gemma!"

There was no reply. Gemma ran up the stairs, shouting his name as she went. Not a sound.

Knocking on his bedroom door she still got no reply, so she opened it and went in.

The first thing she saw was his unmade bed. His room was a mess. A pile of school books were lying in a muddle on the floor, rather as if they had been tipped there. Clothes were pulled out of drawers, it looked as if a whirlwind had been through.

He's gone! Gemma suddenly knew for a certainty that Michael had gone. His books had been dumped from the baggy holdall he always took around with him, and clothes and necessities must have been stuffed in their place. She didn't have to go to the bathroom to know she wouldn't find his toothbrush. He had run away.

Where would he go? Did he have any money? She walked slowly down the stairs. This was a staggering blow, she hadn't thought for a moment he would do this. It was all her fault. He was terrified about the diary – the police would be more certain than ever that he had killed Paul, so he had fled.

She walked automatically into Rita's kitchen. Rita, she knew, would be home soon after one o'clock. She looked at her watch, it was close to one now.

On Rita's kitchen table two cups and saucers were standing ready next to the waiting tea pot. Gemma was mildly surprised. When Rita left the office that morning early she hadn't known that Gemma would be coming over. A page of Rita's phone pad was sticking out, half under the teapot. Gemma picked it up.

Couldn't bear not knowing myself – dashed back. Michael's not here – please don't tell anyone. Will come as soon as I can – bit of a crisis – trying to find out where he's gone. Please wait. Love, R.

So Rita knew Michael had gone and was trying to trace him. She obviously knew how it would look to the police and was worried sick. At least she knew.

That was a weight off Gemma's mind. And knowing that the diary was gone too was a relief. The police might suspect Michael, but they'd never get that. It was clear Rita still didn't know about it.

But it was odd. She had rung Michael soon after eight that morning, and Rita had phoned her the second time close to twelve. What had happened in the four hours in between? Rita must have dashed home after Michael called her, say at nine-thirty, left her message and then, some time later, phoned Gemma again.

Gemma put her hand to her forehead which was starting to ache. Oh, Becca where are you? I need to talk this through with you, come soon, she prayed silently.

Of course she would wait for Rita, but she was so shaken by what had happened to her and so guilty about frightening Michael into this last move, that she desperately needed her friend.

I could phone the police about the fire from here myself, she thought, and went back to the hall where the phone sat on its small table. For a moment she stared at it, hesitating. She pictured Chief Inspector Beale's square face and firm voice. It would be fine if he answered it for he knows about the rat, she thought. In Gemma's mind the dead rat and this last scare were somehow connected.

But what if someone else comes to the phone, what can I say? I thought someone locked me in my room, and started a fire on the terrace? No, I wasn't locked in for long, and no, I wasn't really in danger, just terrified. Are the police interested in things as small as that? Oh, I'll wait for Becca, she decided, and went back to the kitchen.

Gemma, agitated beyond belief, forgot that she was there to try to comfort her aunt, not the other way round. She was relying on Rita's strength to get her through as it had always done.

She took two painkillers from her bag and poured a glass of water. Gulping them down, she carried the glass into the sitting-room, sipping the water as she went.

Why didn't Becca come? The morning paper was lying on Rita's desk. Trying to keep calm, Gemma picked it up. As she did so she dislodged something on the desk that fell on to the carpet with a flutter. It was a piece torn out of a notebook. Gemma picked it up. It was in Michael's writing, an early draft, with alterations here and there, of their secret plans for the "Host a Murder" game.

"Lord Fuss in the cellar," she read, and "Madame Crystal in the dining-room." My place, she mused sadly. I wonder why they changed it all. Without warning sudden tears blurred her vision and she put the paper down. She could picture them all, sitting round Rita's kitchen table. They would be arguing and plotting, and it would be all for her birthday. It seems a lifetime ago, she thought sadly.

Oh, Becca, do come!

For about another quarter of an hour Gemma sat

reading Rita's paper, or really watching the minute hand of her watch creep round to one-thirty. She wandered about and ended up staring out of the kitchen window at Rita's neat garden all tidied up for winter. She saw again the riot of colour it had been in the summer. In the happy months ... when they were all ... before...

I can't stand this, she thought desperately and went to the phone. She dialled her own number and heard the bell ringing in the hall a dozen times before she put the receiver down again.

That means Becca's on her way, she thought thankfully. Gemma opened the front door and looked down the street. There was no sign of Rebecca's striding figure. She returned to the hall and dialled the Peels' house, knowing the number by heart. That, too, rang endlessly on their kitchen dresser. "Oh, where is everybody?" she wailed.

17

In spite of the November chill, Rebecca felt hot and uncomfortable as she rushed from the bus stop to the Old Rectory. She unwound her scarf and hitched her knapsack of books and files further up her shoulders. Half trotting to the front door, she held her key at the ready, turned it in the lock, and walked in.

Something was lying at the foot of the stairs. Something that was shapeless and colourless and seemed to be breathing.

Rebecca's eyes adjusted from the bright light outside to the comparative dimness of the hall. She shut the door and took a step forwards, squinting at it. A sour smell rose to her nostrils.

For a long second she did not realize what it was – then she gave a strangled sort of scream and fell back against the front door.

It was a very old, stinking chicken carcass and it seemed to be breathing because it was smothered in writhing, tumbling maggots. Some of these were moving blindly over the rug and the polished floorboards. Rebecca stepped on a few and felt their small bodies squash beneath her shoe.

"Ugh!" She shuddered from head to foot. Rebecca pulled herself round, opened the door again and staggered out on to the front doorstep, trying not to be sick. She scraped the sole of her shoe on the grass, striving hard to control her urge to retch.

"Gemma!" she thought in alarm and turned to the door again. There she stopped. There was no way she was going to go past those … things! But Gemma! Rebecca gathered her scattered books and knapsack and decided she must go round to the back door to see if it was open and Gemma was home. If she wasn't there, then she must prevent Gemma seeing the carcass at all costs. I hope I'm not too late, she thought, horrified.

Rounding the corner of the house and peering in all directions, Rebecca walked swiftly up the flagged path towards the back door. There she was stopped again, her senses reeling and preparing to leave her. A large untidy cross was painted on the panel of the door, in what looked like blood. Once again her knapsack tumbled off her shoulders.

"Oh, God! What on earth's going on?" She sat down heavily on the path and twisted her wrist.

Beside her slumped body there were red drops on

the flags. Clearly they were the same substance as the cross. Certainly they were red, and from a distance looked like blood, but Rebecca realized, with great relief, they were in fact red paint. She smudged one with a tip of a finger to make certain.

Nothing would make her go into the house by the front, that she knew, but she couldn't leave without making sure Gemma was safely out of it, too. She didn't have a key, but she could use her lungs.

"Gemma!" Rebecca shouted her friend's name as loudly as she could. "Gemma, are you home?"

Not a sound in reply. She took a few steps round the house and tried again. "Gemma!" Rebecca yelled up to the upstairs windows. Still no answering cry.

She moved on round the house shouting Gemma's name and saw the blackened mess on the terrace under Gemma's window.

"My God! What's been going on here? Gemma!" Fear made her voice into a squeak. Gemma was obviously not at home.

Nonplussed and definitely afraid, Rebecca thought of Sam. She would go home at once and find him. This was horrid and had to be sorted out. She hoped Gemma was safe at Rita's house.

Then, with a shock, she realized that Gemma, wherever she was, might return home alone.

Better leave a note for her, she thought. She must be stopped from going inside. She'd put it on the back door.

Tearing a sheet from her file, Rebecca's unsteady

hand picked up a felt tip pen. She rubbed her sore wrist but managed to write a short note. She didn't have a drawing-pin, so she stuck it up on the back door with some sellotape, trying to cover as much of the cross with it as she could. Then she left immediately, breaking into a run. She'd phone Rita's house as soon as she got home.

The watcher was not smiling now, but laughing. How predictable people are, the laughter said.

At half-past two, when neither Rita nor Rebecca had arrived, Gemma despaired. Her nerves were in shreds and her need to talk to someone urgent. The phone shrilled at her, and she jumped out of her skin.

"Hello?" Gemma spoke, her voice sounding strange and tense.

There was no reply. She held it to her ear for a little longer before asking, "Anyone there?"

There was no answer so she replaced the receiver. Immediately it rang again, and again Gemma picked it up.

"This is Rita Palmer's house," she said, in case it was one of Rita's clients trying to reach her. "Can I help?"

Still the earpiece of the phone was quiet and Gemma put it down once more, only to have it blare at her yet again.

For the third time Gemma placed the receiver to her ear. This time she decided not to say anything either and see what happened. She counted. By the time she reached sixty-one she heard a small intake of breath. Someone was there. A tiny voice, like a child's, began to chant,

"*Ladybird, ladybird, fly away home,*
Your house is on fire, your children all gone…"

Then came a wheezing, gasping sound that could only be laughter.

Gemma flung the phone down on its bed as if it was a snake, and stood shaking. She wasn't safe anywhere. Someone knew where she was, someone who also knew about the fire at her home … and the rat … and…

She hurried out, struggling into her coat as she stumbled down the path.

As she turned into the street she heard Rita's phone begin to ring again. Without looking back she walked blindly away.

Where she walked after that Gemma was never sure, but in a state of severe shock and misery she just went on and on down familiar streets without even seeing them. When she came to herself, over an hour later, she was standing staring at the large pond in the local park not far from her house.

Where had she been? Part of her mind reminded her she had stood at Rebecca's front door, pressing the bell for a long time, but had she really done that? If she had, no one answered.

The afternoon light dimmed and turned to a dull gold, making the surface of the pond look like molten metal. Sea birds, far inland, wheeled and cried, and the air began to cut like a knife, a foretaste of the hard frost to come.

Gemma's frozen mind was beyond thinking.

"East, West, home's best... East, West..." she chanted aloud, and, longing for her father's strong, comforting presence, she let her feet take her there.

Gemma slipped into the garden by the side gate and went to the back door. She looked at Rebecca's note with dull incomprehension. Then she saw it was stuck in the centre of a red, painted cross. She touched the paint with her finger; it was still wet.

"Gem," she read, "don't go in. There's something unpleasant going on and you shouldn't go in on your own. I'm off to find Sam, go to Tracy's and I'll see you there. R."

At first the words made no sense to Gemma's numb mind. She read them over and over. Perhaps it wasn't Rebecca's note. It was hard to tell from the heavy felt-tip printing, wobbly from Rebecca's hurt wrist.

Someone else could have left this note, she thought, not Becca. She felt icy cold. Not the cold of winter, but the cold of fear. She was certain now that she was in danger.

She read the note again, but it still didn't make a lot of sense.

The rat in her fridge came back to haunt her. The memory didn't make things any better. She tried so hard to blot that memory out at Rita's house, when it first returned to her, its implications were horrible. But now she couldn't push it away, its bloody head and the look of its stiff, matted body rose in front of her, clearly etched, and her stomach heaved.

No, she couldn't go inside now. Something might be waiting for her in there. Something much worse than a dead rat... Or someone...

Gemma was trembling, she had to lean against the back door for support. A nightmare, that's what it was ... why couldn't she wake up?

The note said "Go to Tracy's" but she wouldn't do that. How was she to know that wasn't a trick? Who could she trust now? Besides, Tracy may not be at home – nobody was at home.

She must try to think. It was as if all her reactions had gone into slow motion.

Something hard struck her in the centre of her chest and her heart nearly stopped with fright. Whatever it was fell at her feet with a slight rattle. She looked down and saw a largish stone wrapped around with something looking like crumpled paper.

Gemma stared around her into the gathering dusk. How did it get there? Was it thrown at her? Nothing moved, she couldn't see anything or any-body. She bent down and picked it up.

The paper wrapped around the stone was very crumpled and dirty but Gemma saw that it was written on in faint pencil. She tried to make it out.

Jet neds yu cum now.

In her state of shock and fear, she realized it had to

be from Roach. Jet needed her, and she was almost forgetting about her promise. That's where she would go. She'd be safe there, no one would think of looking for her in the old empty church.

She nearly got a biro out of her bag to write where she was going on the bottom of the note, but she stopped herself. Better not do anything to reveal where she was.

Gemma felt like a hunted animal. Waifs together, she thought sadly.

Her eyes looked up at the blind windows of her home, dark and silent, and now barred to her. It was no longer her refuge, the familiar place of safety and comfort; it loomed above her full of menace.

Feeling totally unreal, Gemma turned away.

18

By the time Rebecca had reached her own house, Sam had left. There was a gap in his row of tapes so Rebecca knew he had been there already and taken the ones he wanted. Oh, Sam! Rebecca cried inwardly, she needed him. Gemma was God knows where, and nasty things were being done in her house. She wanted to return there, to clean up before Gemma saw the mess, but needed Sam's company and strength. She couldn't do it alone.

"Where is he?" Rebecca went through the possibilities. Then she began some urgent telephoning.

No one had answered the phone at Rita's house when she phoned there before. She tried it for the second time. Still no one was in.

Tracy was mildly surprised when Rebecca called her. No, she hadn't seen Gemma or Sam that day.

They had no plans to meet until the early evening. Guy was coming round to pick her up.

"Please," said Rebecca, "could you stay in for a while longer in case Gemma sees my note before I can find her."

Tracy, a bit mystified, agreed to send Guy on ahead and wait for a call.

Guy was out.

In desperation, Rebecca looked up the number of the supermarket Sam worked in. She knew the Christian name of one of his colleagues there, Damian. Perhaps she could get to speak to him.

She was in luck. She did.

He told her Sam had called there and gone off to a café with another friend, whose hours were more flexible than his.

Yes, he agreed, it was probably the one they all used, Jack's Diner.

Rebecca sighed with relief, thanked him, seized her coat, and praying that Sam would still be there, dashed out.

Gemma, feeling like a fugitive from everything she knew and loved, dragged at the old orchard door until it was open enough for her to squeeze through. Then, covering the few metres of uneven ground before the graveyard began, she sprinted to the church. It loomed above her head and shut out some of the remaining light with its bulk.

She went, more stealthily, round to the side door

where she paused nervously and tried to make out if there was any sound coming from within. She couldn't hear a thing, and with a sense of having done all this before, tapped softly.

From where she stood, she could just see the higher windows of the Old Rectory. She looked at them with longing, wondering painfully if its familiar rooms would ever offer her sanctuary again.

Gemma knocked on the door a second time, a little louder.

Cautiously the door opened a crack. Roach's ferrety nose peered out. He opened the door wider when he saw her, and let her in.

It was completely dark in the vestry, and the musty smell from the old stones, cats and damp assailed her more strongly than she remembered. As did the cold. She shivered violently, and still in a state of shock, longed for the light and sun of an hour or so ago. No candles were lit. She couldn't make out the shape of anything much around her. The floor seemed empty of bedding and bags. It was quite clear.

The door that led into the rest of the building from the vestry was open, showing a small amount of thin light, which told Gemma that it would be easier to see in the body of the church.

A sudden sense of panic seized her. I hate it in here, I can't stay, her instincts shouted, I've got to get out.

She turned round quickly to go back, but Roach was standing close behind and she bumped into him.

" 'Ere," he said, laying a hand on her shoulder and

turning her back again. "That's the way, keep going. Jet's waiting for ya."

Gemma expected to find Jet lying on one of their sleeping bags, resting her ankle. As she obviously wasn't, perhaps there was somewhere more comfortable in the church itself.

Smothering her moment of panic, she shrugged off Roach's hand and went on through the door.

The large cavity of the church seen in slightly better light gave Gemma some relief. She looked around her. The building was just an outer shell. It had been built in the familiar convention of early Victorian churches, when the Gothic tradition had returned with a vengeance.

The huge space of the nave was empty of its pews. No vestige remained of the rood screen or the organ, and where the altar once stood under the large triple windows, too large to get boarded up, was nothing at all. Only the two steps up to the dais which once held it were still there. The steps where for decades worshippers had mounted and knelt to take Holy Communion.

Even the pulpit had been removed along with the smaller altars in the two side chapels. Dust hung in the air so thickly, Gemma could almost feel it parting to let her through.

She tried to pierce the gloom, staring about her.

"Jet?" Gemma called softly.

"Belt up," Roach said in her ear, "don't wake the neighbours."

She was being led towards the rear of the church, towards the cavity where, long ago, a curtain had hung to hide the alcove where the bell-ringers climbed the wooden stairs to the belfry.

Then, as if at a given signal, Roach seized her from behind, pinning her elbows together and making her cry out.

"What is this … ow … Roach … let go!"

He turned her bodily to face the opening in the stone wall.

"Up we go!" He shoved her forward and just stopped her falling head first over the bottom step as she staggered.

"I said, up!"

"Stop it … ow … that hurts! Jet!"

Roach, behind her back, kneed her and snorted. Gemma's heart quailed. It sounded like a laugh. If Roach was laughing … then, it was probable that Jet…?

"Help!" Gemma opened her lungs and yelled.

Roach looped one steely arm through her bent elbows, and used the other to reach out for her mouth. His hand clamped over it and he kneed her again.

"Shut it!" There was no mistaking the menace in his harsh whisper.

Gemma realized she was helpless in his grasp. Her slight frame was bent over double, he was far too strong for her to resist and she knew it.

There wasn't a choice; she went up. Her terrified

mind was racing, trying to think. In the end she gave up. It was hard enough to concentrate on taking each step at a time; the stairs were narrow, made of wood and not very firm.

At last they reached the bell-ringers' platform. This spanned the tower in the days when there were ringers to ring the bells. Then the platform was no doubt kept in good order. It was a different story now. The supporting beams for the floor were still in place, but the floorboards covering at least one third of the platform were missing. It looked to Gemma as if the planks had been levered up and carefully removed. They were stacked neatly against one side of the tower. There was a coil of rope beside them.

What was infinitely worse and made her gasp was the way the exposed joists had been treated. Someone had sawed them through in two places, removing the middle of each one to leave a yawning, empty space.

It looks prepared, her faltering mind told her.

Roach, with one more vicious knee in her spine, pushed her on to the remaining platform, letting go his grasp at the same time.

Gemma staggered forward on to her knees, putting out her hands to break her fall. The old planks shuddered beneath her weight and a splinter entered one of her fingers.

"Hi, Gemma." Jet, leaning against the opposite wall of the tower, looked at her calmly. "By the way, the ankle's better – thought you'd like to know." She held out one of her black-booted legs and shook it.

"Jet?" Gemma tried to get to her feet, but her knees were so wobbly she fell back again. She sucked a bead of blood from her finger.

"The same," Jet said, glancing at her watch. It was set in a thick leather band on her wrist. Then she added, "Well, not quite the same."

Gemma didn't know what she meant.

"Why are you doing this? What have I ever done to you?"

"You?" A cruel little smile lifted the corner of Jet's mouth. She was studying Gemma rather like a technician studies an experimental rabbit before he makes the first injection.

"You've done nothing *to* me. It's what you're going to do *for* me that I'm interested in."

Roach snorted again; he thought Jet was very witty. Gemma didn't see the joke.

"Let me go, you can't hold me here. It's ridiculous, I'll be missed."

"Oh yeah?" Jet was still smiling. "Your friend rushed off just now as if Old Nick was after her. She won't be back in a hurry. They won't find you for a bit."

Another shockwave hit Gemma.

"You've been watching us!"

"Said I would, didn' I? Maybe a bit different from what you thought."

Roach was standing in the narrow doorway,

guarding it in case Gemma tried to run. He wiped his nose with the back of his hand and kept sniggering.

Gemma began to struggle to her feet. She was trying hard to think logically. If she could stand up she'd feel better. There was a reason for all this – she had to find what it was.

Jet watched her until she was nearly upright. Then she stepped forward and shoved Gemma casually in the centre of her chest, pushing her off balance and back to the floor again.

"Oh, don't go," she said. "We want you, don't we, Roach?"

Gemma felt trapped now and very frightened. In spite of all her efforts to prevent it, she began to tremble. Jet watched her, and came in for the kill.

There was no sign of the shivering waif, who Gemma had felt so sorry for, now. Her dark eyes in her white face glittered with malice.

She stood over Gemma's defenceless body for a moment, relishing her power, feeling good as Gemma flinched away. Then she squatted down beside her and stared into her face.

"It's like this, see, Gemma. You're a nice kid. You tried to help Roach and me, didn't you? Giving us food and that. Well, we're grateful, we like you and we want to be mates, more than mates."

Gemma stayed silent. She held herself together as best she could, waiting for what was to follow and trying to assimilate the change in Jet.

It was shocking. The waif down on her luck,

trying to cope with what fate threw at her, was gone. In her place was a dangerous power-mad fury from a horror film.

"Let's play a game," Jet went on. "Let's play *sharing*. Know that one?"

Her face was very close to Gemma's and her dark eyes looked into Gemma's blue ones with a frightening intensity.

Jet waited while her words reached Gemma's consciousness.

"Sharing?" Gemma repeated without understanding.

"Yeah, sharing. It goes like this, see. You always wanted to help Roach and me, didn't ya? Well, now you can. You can start sharing. See?"

Gemma didn't. Her expression said so.

Jet reached into her inside jacket pocket and drew out a piece of paper. She turned it round so that Gemma could see there was writing on it.

"No, we haven't got much time," she said, still softly. "So there's no room for silly babies. What I want is for you to put your name to this. Then Roach and me will take care of you. We can all scarper together, and no one will know. You'll be safe with us, quite safe. You won't be getting any more … horrid frights, Gemma."

Oh, God, Gemma thought. The rat!

"What is this paper?" she asked.

Jet dangled it in front of Gemma, but she couldn't read it.

"It's an IOU, simple," Jet said. "You're rich, right? You came into a lot of money when your mum and dad died. Well, this paper says you want to share some of it with your very good friends. Got it? You owe it them."

With her other hand, she produced a biro. "Only we got to move now. Just sign on the dotted, make it quick."

"You're mad!" Gemma knew now it was a fact. "I don't owe you a thing. I don't even know you!"

Jet's eyes blazed at her. "Listen, narkhead, you owe me and I'll tell you why. I lost my mum, right? And you lost yours. Yours was rich, mine didn't have a cent. Well, we're going to even that up.

Sign this, NOW!" Jet held the paper out with one hand and a biro in the other, looking at her watch again as she did so.

With hands shaking visibly, Gemma took the paper and looked at it. It was not very long and was written in a large, spiky hand.

High up in the tower walls were the two windows that Gemma could see from her bedroom window. These shed the only light that was getting through to the platform. It was like a shadow of light rather than a beam, but Gemma was just able to make out the words.

She read it aloud. "This is to certify that I, Gemma Davies, owe Pauline Dodgeson – who's she?"

"Never mind that, just sign, come on!" Jet said roughly.

186

"That's your real name: Pauline Dodgeson," Gemma said, wondering what the rush was about.

"Get on," Roach broke in. "We got to go!"

Jet cuffed Gemma on the side of her face.

"Go on, sign. We haven't got all night." She looked at her watch again.

"… the sum of £10,000, which is her right to have." Gemma put her hand up to her cuffed cheek. There was a space for Gemma's name and the date had been written in already.

"Roach'll make his mark when you've done."

Anger began to rise in Gemma, pushing her fear to the background. She looked at Jet's pasty, gloating face and her figure in its shabby black garments, at her spiky hair and dirty hands, and wondered why she ever thought she looked pathetic. Then she turned to look at Roach, mean and cruel and very greedy. Suddenly she surprised herself by laughing.

Her laughter was short-lived.

Jet brought her hand back and hit Gemma a swingeing blow on her mouth. It split her bottom lip, making blood ooze out in a trickle down her chin. Bright lights flashed behind Gemma's eyes, and she covered her face with her hands.

Jet gripped her arm on one side and, at her signal, Roach came up and gripped her arm on the other. They dragged her to the edge of the platform where the planks had been removed. It wasn't far to go, the space was small.

Together, they made her bend forward, so that her

head was protruding over the edge of the platform and she was totally in their hands. Gemma found herself staring down to the tiled floor of the church, a long way below.

Jet hissed in her ear, "You're going to end it all here and now, or you're going to sign. It's as simple as that, Gemma. You want to end it all anyway, don't you? Tried to do it the other night, didn't you? All those sleeping pills you took. You shouldn't drink so much chocolate. We saw the doctor come and she'll tell. You couldn't stand the heat any more. Your precious Michael's in schtuck for killing one of your friends, and you don't have a mummy and a daddy any more to protect you. Poor little rich girl, what's the point of going on?"

The cruel words went on and on. With her head still reeling from Jet's blow, Gemma heard her own breath leave her lungs in short, harsh, terrified gasps. All she was aware of was the dark space looming below her.

Jet's voice dropped to a low croon, "Signing's a doddle, signing'll make it all go away ... so let's get it over..."

There was a crash somewhere far below, and a sound of scrabbling followed by running footsteps.

"Gemma?" A voice penetrated the cold and dark spaces.

"Gemma, are you in here?"

Sam, breathed Gemma. Oh, Sam!

She drew in her breath to try to shout, but Roach's

hand clamped over it once more. She was dragged from the edge of the platform and pulled tightly back against Roach's chest as he leant against the tower wall. She felt as if she was in a vice, unable to move or scream. They stood bonded together in deep shadow.

"Keep her quiet," hissed Jet and went quickly down the stairs.

19

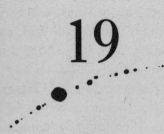

Sam and Rebecca stood in the centre of the large nave, trying to make out the terrain. They could hardly see a thing.

Sam was at Jack's Diner when Rebecca got there, and together they dashed back to the Old Rectory. On the way Rebecca told Sam about Gemma's rendezvous in the old church and about the two squatters. She also told Sam about her own experiences. Sam's face grew grim as he listened.

They entered the house by the front. Rebecca was clinging to Sam's hand and trying to ignore the way her shoes slid on the bodies of the maggots that were still writhing round the carcass.

On the kitchen table they found Gemma's old message, the one she had left when she had fled to Rita's earlier. As no one had answered Rebecca's two phone calls there, they decided to go to the church to see if Gemma had kept her appointment. If not they could ask the squatters if they had seen her.

Sam wasn't able to open the side door by the lock, but both of them thrust their weight against the old timbers until it gave at its hinges and they tumbled into the vestry.

"There's someone here, Bec." Sam was listening hard. "I heard something."

"Look, Sam!" Rebecca clutched his arm in apprehension. She saw a flicker of yellow light coming towards them from the rear of the church.

They turned to meet it. Jet was holding a candle in one hand, shielding its flame with the other. She always carried one about with her, and had lit it on her way down.

"Is that Jet?" Rebecca spoke tentatively; she had only seen Jet's back view once, going away down the garden.

"Yeah? Who wants to know?"

"I'm Rebecca, Gemma's friend. This is my brother, Sam."

As Jet didn't say anything, Rebecca went on hurriedly, "We're looking for Gemma, have you seen her?"

"Why?" Jet asked. "Not exactly her scene, is it? In trouble, is she?"

"No-o," Rebecca answered. "But she..."

"There was a bit of a fire at your place earlier. She put it out. You share with her, don't you?"

"Fire!" Rebecca remembered the remains of the bonfire on the terrace.

"Yeah, I nearly went to give a hand, but she got it sorted."

"Look," Sam broke in. "You didn't by any chance see anyone lurking near the house, did you? You don't happen to have a pot of red paint handy?"

"Me?" Jet looked surprised and innocent.

"I'm sorry to ask, Jet," Rebecca said, not wanting Sam to get too strong with her, "but we're at our wits' end. We hoped Gemma was here, you see, she said she was coming. We've tried everywhere else."

"Well, see for yourselves, she's not. And, I might add, I don't like your implication. What paint?"

The candlelight flickered round Jet's face as she spoke. It looked disembodied and Rebecca shivered.

"How's your ankle?" Sam asked, staring at her.

"Better," Jet answered him shortly, staring back.

"Well, OK," she said then, as if making up her mind to tell them something important. "Gemma was here, about half an hour ago. I asked her to come. I saw someone creeping round the back of your house the night before last. Acting suspicious. Whoever it was was there again today and I thought she ought to know."

Sam and Rebecca looked at each other. That was the night they'd had the row, the night Gemma had slept so deeply.

"What were they doing?" Sam asked.

"Looked to me like they was watching and waiting, they kept going round, peering in the windows. I don't know if they got in in the end, I didn't wait to see. Too cold. Look, I've got to go. Roach an' me are off out of this now, we got to get going."

Sam said, "OK, Jet. Sorry you've been bothered. Come on, Becca."

Reluctantly, Rebecca followed him out through the damaged vestry door.

"Oh, Sam, where can she be?" Rebecca asked this question without expecting him to answer. "This was my last hope. I knew we'd planned to come here together, but I suppose I hoped…"

They began to walk slowly away from the church.

"I know this much." Sam's voice was deep and firm with determination. Gemma's wealth had faded completely from his thoughts of her. All he wanted was to see her sweet face laughing with him, warm and happy. "There's something very nasty going on. If anyone hurts her, or touches a hair on her head, they'll have me to deal with, and that's a promise!"

Up in the belfry Gemma strained against Roach's chest, but the arm that held her to him was like a steel band. She couldn't shift it.

With mounting desperation she heard her friends' voices far below, and Jet's in answer to them.

When she realized that they were leaving the church, and that she would be left again with these two utterly merciless people, her fear made her crazy.

She raised her foot – why hadn't she done it before? – and brought it backwards and down hard against Roach's shin.

He gasped and for a brief second the hand over her mouth shifted enough to let her get hold of some of it in her teeth.

She bit him, and had the satisfaction of feeling her teeth meet together through a soft pleat in his palm.

Roach cursed, and Gemma was free long enough to open her lungs and yell, "Sam!" at the top of her voice, before Roach's now bloody hand clamped over her mouth again.

Jet took the stairs two at a time, put the candle down, and, as Roach held Gemma, punched her in the stomach. She had lost the game, she had to finish and get out fast, they were late.

"Roach! Too late for anything now. We get rid of her. Over you go!" she hissed in Gemma's face. She looked as if killing Gemma would give her as much pleasure as getting hold of her money – probably more.

They dragged the helpless, winded girl to the open gap once more.

This is it, thought Gemma quite clearly, gulping in air. Better not to look. She shut her eyes. Just think of something good... Her mum and dad... Michael... Sam. She waited, suspended for the final push.

It didn't come.

"Let her go!" Loud and commanding, Sam's voice rose up to them. "We know she's there and we can see you both. Let her go at once!"

This was almost true. From way below the half-dismantled platform, only Gemma's head and torso and the legs of her two captors could be faintly seen.

He heard me! Gemma breathed.

On the platform no one moved.

"Make any move at all, and I'll push her over," Jet shouted.

She picked up the length of rope and, with Gemma helpless in Roach's arms, tied her hands behind her back tightly.

"Sam, help! Sam!" Gemma shrieked and struggled furiously.

Hysteria was very close.

Roach pushed her to the ground and Jet bound her legs.

"If she falls," Sam yelled, beside himself and not knowing what to do, "you'll both get it. We are witnesses, my sister and I. You'll never get out of jail!" He was shouting so loudly, his voice cracked.

Gemma continued to scream and struggle, help was so near...

"Stop her, for God's sake," Jet flung at Roach, but it was all he could do to hold the thrashing girl.

"I'll do it, then, braindead! Give me your neck-cloth."

She pulled the unsavoury piece of cloth from his neck and bound it round Gemma's head and mouth, pulled it tightly and knotted it. It was an efficient gag.

"Now," she turned on her accomplice, "go down there and sort them out fast, we haven't got any time left!"

Roach left the platform.

Gemma, bound and gagged, fell silent and limp, exhausted, with all fight leaving her.

"Go for help, Bec," Sam said, to where he hoped Rebecca stood. It was now almost too dark to see her. She was shouting up to Gemma, trying to comfort her.

"Right! Oh, Sam, be careful, don't do anything daft!"

"Go!"

Rebecca began to make her way to the vestry door.

Without warning she was grasped from behind by a strong, muscular arm and a voice in her ear hissed, "Tell your precious brother to shut up, or you'll have it!" Something sharp pricked her neck.

"Oh God, a knife, he's got a knife, Sam!" Terrified, Rebecca screamed. The point of the knife pressed harder.

"Shut it you! Now listen both..."

Roach never got the next word out, for Sam, doing his best imitation of a bullet yet, tackled him round his knees and he fell hard. They heard his head crack against the tiled floor. Then there was nothing more to hear.

"Roach?" Jet's voice came floating down to them.

She had heard the encounter and was getting a nasty feeling about it.

"Sam, Sam," Rebecca cried in real distress. "My hand … his knife must have cut it … it's bleeding!"

"For God's sake, not now, Bec. Hold on, can't you? Just hold on! Don't look!" Sam sounded frantic.

But it was no use, Rebecca's own darkness became darker than the one outside her, and she fainted. She lay full length on the floor of the old church, beside the stunned figure of her attacker.

"Brilliant," Sam groaned.

There was no sound from the platform. He pressed his hands to his forehead and thought hard. Jet was up there with Gemma and he was down here alone. He didn't think much of his chances of rushing her before she tipped Gemma over the edge, and he couldn't leave them alone to go for help. He was stumped.

20

"Get your hands off me!"

Sam started. He had noticed nothing new.

"Let me go, damn you!" It was definitely not Gemma's voice but it came from the platform.

"What's going on?" he shouted, not expecting an answer.

To his astonishment he realized that the protests were coming from Jet. Someone was up on the platform gripping her in much the same way that Gemma had been held. Like Gemma, she was being pulled forward to bend perilously over the waiting gap in the floor. He watched in amazement as she tried ineffectually to struggle.

Sam hadn't heard anyone come in. It must have been when he was rescuing Rebecca from Roach. It was dark enough for a whole army to arrive and no one notice. He hoped whoever it was was on Gemma's side.

He could just make out the silhouette of Jet's head by the light dimly shining through the small tower windows. The faint glow back-lit the figures he could discern from the ground. He listened, amazed, to hear shouts of rage and fear.

"Say another word, you, and it'll be your last!"

Rita's voice!

"Rita!" Sam bellowed. "Is that you?"

"What do you think you're doing?" gasped Jet, realizing that she had met her match for strength. Rita had spent a lifetime lifting and supporting people in her job. She was very strong.

"Sam!" Rita's voice was strong and clear. "Glad you're here."

"Feeling's mutual," Sam said back, meaning it. He was aware of a rustling sound somewhere near his feet.

"Bec? You OK?" There was a slight moan, but no one answered.

"Go for the police, would you?" Rita shouted. "I've got this one, have you seen the other?"

"You narkhead!" Jet was screaming again. "She's the one behind all this... You don't want to believe..."

Rita jerked her roughly back.

"Come down!" shouted Sam. "We can sort it out easier on the ground."

"No, no, you got to listen to me." Jet sounded mad

with panic and rage. "It was her, I tell you. She made me do it. She wanted Gemma out the way. It's all her idea!"

"Don't listen, Sam," urged Rita. "She'll say anything."

But Jet was still shouting desperately. "She gave me the layout of the rooms, and the keys – how'd you think I knew what pills she took? I knew where the fridge was, an' all!"

"Shut up – you're raving!" Rita screamed at her. "She nearly murdered Gemma, Sam, you saw her!"

Rita must have been here watching silently, Sam thought with a cold realization. I wonder how long for?

"I will tell, I will!" Jet could not be stopped. Rita's strength was enough to hold her but not to silence her. Not unless she pushed her over the edge as Jet had threatened to push Gemma.

"She planned it all. With Gemma out the way, we could all have a bit. She's next in line, see, she and Michael."

Michael!

In her corner, helpless and bound, Gemma closed her eyes. The nightmare was taking over. Rita... Michael... Jet. All for her money? It could not be true, it was some hideously awful dream.

"Listen, for God's sake, Gemma." Rita turned her head and spoke directly to her for the first time. "She's telling a pack of dreadful lies. She's one of my problem cases. Her brother's simple and when her mum died the landlord threw them out. Not surprising, Jet has a history of violence. She's bordering on schizophrenic! They came up here from London, and we tried to help. Then they disappeared. I had a tip-off they were here."

Why doesn't Rita untie my hands? Gemma thought numbly. I love her, I believe her. Jet's evil.

Jet tore herself free from Rita's grasp with a giant effort. Instead of shouting down to Sam, or trying to escape, she flung herself beside Gemma and grabbed her shoulders.

"I made a mistake, see," she spat at Gemma, her eyes black with hate. Gemma shrank away as far as her bonds could let her. "I thought that guy in the red dress and the silly hat was you! Rita said you'd be in red. She told me where to wait. In the bedroom wardrobe, she said, and you'd turn up, but she got it wrong.

"YOU GOT IT WRONG, RITA!" Jet shouted, shaking Gemma hard between her hands. Her shout reverberated from wall to wall.

"*He* turned up there instead," she went on as if there had been no interruption. "And I hit him in the dark. He had blond hair and all. I didn't know, blast it!"

Gemma's head swam under the shaking, and dark rings around her vision threatened to wipe out her sight and send her into oblivion. I want to die. Why can't I just die? she moaned silently.

Listening below, utterly shell-shocked, Sam was rooted to the spot.

He felt someone reaching for his arm.

"Bec?"

"Hmm," she spoke a little shakily.

"Well enough to get help now?" he whispered to her urgently, every nerve tense.

"I'm off," Rebecca said, getting her bearings. She felt bitterly cold and was shivering with shock, but understood what she had to do. She left as fast as she could go, and headed for a telephone.

Rita sprang on Jet. This time the girl couldn't escape from her strong hands and arms.

"You bungled it, and now you're trying to pull a fast one on me and Michael, you rat!"

Rita hit her, and as Jet reeled, grabbed her again.

"I heard what you were doing with that IOU. You thought you could run before I came – pathetic!"

She dragged Jet back to the gaping hole in the floor.

"Two-timing double-crossers get what's coming to them. Look down there!"

She gave the petrified girl an enormous shove and Jet, arms waving, screaming terribly, plunged to the floor many metres below.

Her screams were cut off in mid-cry as she thudded on to the floor.

For a count of five, the old church resounded to the violence and the noise. It had happened so fast.

Horrified, Sam ran forward to where Jet lay face down on the chipped tiles. Kneeling beside her, he watched, aghast. Even in the gloom he could see a black stain slowly beginning to spread around her head.

"Rita!" he yelled with what voice he had left, but he didn't think she would answer him. Not now.

He was right.

Up on the platform, she was bending over Gemma, undoing her bonds. She took off the gag last of all, and stood back.

Gemma tried to get up. She was shaking with terror and fright and was very, very shocked. Rita bent to help her.

Gemma felt her aunt's warm hands supporting her, lifting her to her feet, and looked into the familiar face. Rita smiled at her. Slowly, Gemma smiled back. Everything was all right now, Rita was here. With her head shaken so badly by Jet and all she'd suffered, Gemma had left reality behind her five minutes ago.

Rita was talking to her. Her voice was soft and affectionate. "You love Michael, Gemma dear, don't you?"

Gemma nodded at her, still smiling.

"Well, I love him too, more than anyone, more than myself and … much, much more than you."

Michael, thought Gemma, dear Michael…

"You know he never murdered anyone, don't you? You heard what she said. They'll find him and bring him home and everything will be all right."

Gemma, still smiling, nodded at her.

"I had hoped it would all be different, dear. Easier. But I made a mistake, my plan went wrong, and now

I have to put it right." She had her arm round Gemma's waist, and drew her slowly forward.

"You see, Beryl had it all, always. You're very like her, you know. Then when she died, you had it all and Michael and I got nothing. It has always been the same." Rita's bedside voice went on, soothing Gemma, calming her. "I worked and struggled and you had it easy. Well, you could see it couldn't go on. I couldn't stand by while my Michael had to struggle and Gemma had it easy, could I, Beryl love?"

To Sam below, her voice sounded low and indistinct. He was straining his ears to listen, uncertain about what to do. Should he go up? Or would that make it worse for Gemma?

Suddenly Rita and Gemma appeared at the edge of the platform, and he stiffened.

"This way…"

Sam could hear Rita's words now.

"This way you go and I go, and Michael gets it all. Goodbye, Gemma, darling." She turned around to kiss Gemma on her cheek.

"My God!" he cried. "They're going over together!"

Sam didn't stop to think about his chances of success. He raced for the stairs to the tower, shouting at the top of his voice, "STOP, RITA!"

Rita, startled by Sam's shout, paused for a second before making her final move.

Sam burst on to the platform, grabbed Gemma from behind and drew her away from the edge.

"Rita!" Sam shouted again, but Rita didn't stop.

She threw back her head and with a great cry of "Michael!" that rebounded from the old church's rafters, flung herself over the edge.

Her body landed close to the spot where Jet had fallen. One of her arms flung out to lie across the body of the dead girl.

In Sam's arms Gemma slipped thankfully into unconsciousness.

A deadly silence fell over the church. Somewhere in the distance police sirens were wailing. On the platform, Sam clutched hold of Gemma as if he would never let her go again.

Roach, recovered from his fall, was kneeling beside Jet's still body, weeping, and trying to stroke her spiky hair.

Then Rebecca ran in, shouting "Sam! Gemma!"

"Up here," Sam called to her. In a few moments she was on the platform with them. Between them they carried Gemma slowly and carefully down from the bell-ringers' mutilated platform.

There was a thunderous banging on the main church door, and then a shout as one of the arriving policemen found the open vestry door. Four police officers ran in to the church, torches blazing.

Sudden light blinded the little group as they reached the floor of the church. Two officers went at once to the still, broken figures on the floor. One felt their pulses and another began talking into his radio-link. A third took charge of Roach.

The sergeant turned to look down at Gemma who was lying on the tiles with her head in Rebecca's lap. Her face was very white, and her eyes were shut.

"Is she all right? What on earth's been going on in here?" he asked Sam. "Did one of you telephone?"

"I did," said Rebecca.

"We know who murdered Paul," blurted Sam. "Paul Oliver," he went on, seeing the sergeant's questioning look. The policeman's eyebrows shot up.

"We'll take your statements at the hospital," he said. "It can all wait till then."

Sam put his anorak over Gemma, and now the worst was over, he, too, began to shiver.

Two ambulances came quickly. Jet and Rita were carried swiftly away in the first one, and the others, with Gemma, went together in the second.

They were taken to the casualty ward in the local hospital, and given hot sweet drinks while they gave their statements to the police. Then Sam and Rebecca were gathered up by their parents and taken home.

Gemma was to be kept in for observation for a night at least. She had been through a terrifying ordeal and needed rest and care.

The worst night of their lives was over.

21

"Stay here as long as you like, Gemma dear."
Sam and Rebecca's mother was speaking a few days later.

Rebecca nodded vigorously, and Sam said, "Yes, Gem, do."

Gemma smiled at them both. She felt safe there. Rebecca and Sam's parents had taken her under their wings on her return from hospital. She had badly needed a refuge.

"Take it one day at a time," they advised her. "It will be like learning to walk again."

A shadow passed across her face. Still very pale, the purple smudges under her eyes stood out clearer than ever.

Michael, she thought.

He was often in her mind. When he fled he had

taken a train to Scotland with the only money he possessed. For one bitter night he lived rough. In the morning he turned himself in at a Glasgow police station.

When the police learned his name they told him he was cleared of all suspicion of Paul's murder. They also told him, as kindly as they could, who had done it, and what had happened to his mother. He was kept in hospital overnight, very shocked, and then he insisted on going home alone.

Paul's funeral had come and gone, and Rita's funeral had been a very quiet affair. Gemma had been advised by Dr Peel not to go, fearing the stress would be too great for her. Michael had been her only family mourner, but the solicitor, Hugh Pine, turned up unexpectedly to give him support.

Gemma's heart went out to him in pity as she remembered how he came back to the Peels' house for tea afterwards. Thinner and paler than ever and so quiet and withdrawn.

She wrote him a letter and told him all about Paul's diary and what she had done to it. She begged him to forgive her for frightening him so that he fled on that awful day. She told him that she loved him.

He didn't answer. A few days later she heard that his doctor had sent him to a psychiatric clinic. She hoped it would give him the help he needed. She felt powerless to change things for him.

What is he thinking? Gemma agonized over that. Does he think I believe he was in on Rita's plot? Or does he hate me because he thinks it was somehow all my fault?

She rang him at the clinic every day but the conversations were one-sided. Michael's depression went deep. If she mentioned a visit, he put her off. She had talked to Hugh Pine and he said he would meet Michael when he was better and talk about his future in the family business, her business.

And Rita? Gemma's feelings were still numb where she was concerned. She had loved her. She seemed to be the most stable of people, caring and totally reliable.

With a heavy heart she learned the truth.

The details of Rita's elaborate plotting were slowly being understood. Roach was talking. How, on learning of Michael's flight, she had alerted Jet to make sure Gemma visited the church so they could finish what they had begun. Jet had been given a free rein to do all the unpleasant things she did to Gemma. To frighten and unsettle her. She enjoyed it, obviously.

Rita had used Jet and her brother with promises of financial help and a place to live. But would Rita have ever felt safe with those two still alive...?

Jet had had her own idea about her reward: death, and she had turned out to be right.

Above all, Gemma remembered Rita's distraught, agonized face when Michael was under close suspicion. Her plans had gone terribly wrong.

"Gemma?" Sam's voice brought her back to them. "What are you thinking?"

She smiled at him and reached out her hand to put it on his arm. Since the awful night in the church, all barriers were down between them. He watched over her so carefully; so did Becca. She was a lucky girl.

"I was thinking that when I get my exams over, I'll find the best course I can for business management, and," she went on, watching their faces, "I shall put my house on the market."

"Are you sure?" Rebecca asked her a little anxiously.

"I'm positive. It's time to move forward again. But not too quickly. Christmas is coming, perhaps we can all go on holiday together? Perhaps Michael will be well enough, too, like old times. Let's plan, OK?"

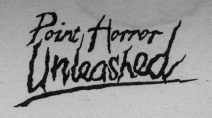

CALLING ALL POINT HORROR FANS!

Welcome to the new wave of fear. If you were
scared before, you'll be *terrified* now...

Transformer
Philip Gross

Look into the eyes of the night...

The Carver
Jenny Jones

The first cut is the deepest...

Blood Sinister
Celia Rees

Cursed be he who looks inside...

At Gehenna's Door
Peter Beere

Abandon hope...

Look out for:
The Vanished
Celia Rees

Point Horror Unleashed.
It's one step beyond...

Point Horror

Dare you read

NIGHTMARE HALL

Where college is a
scream!

**High on a hill overlooking Salem University
hidden in shadows and shrouded in
mystery, sits Nightingale Hall.**

**Nightmare Hall, the students call it.
Because that's where the terror began...**

Don't miss these spine-tingling thrillers:

P●INT CRiME

If you like Point Horror, you'll love Point Crime!

Kiss of Death
School for Death
Peter Beere

Avenging Angel
Break Point
Deadly Inheritance
Final Cut
Shoot the Teacher
The Beat:
Missing Person
Black and Blue
Smokescreen
Asking For It
Dead White Male
Losers
David Belbin

Baa Baa Dead Sheep
Dead Rite
Jill Bennett

A Dramatic Death
Bored to Death
Margaret Bingley

Driven to Death
Patsy Kelly
Investigates:
A Family Affair
End of the Line
No Through Road
Accidental Death
Brotherly Love
Anne Cassidy

Overkill
Alane Ferguson

Deadly Music
Dead Ringer
Death Penalty
Dennis Hamley

Fade to Black
Stan Nicholls

Concrete Evidence
The Alibi
The Smoking Gun
Lawless and Tilley:
The Secrets of the Dead
Deep Waters
Malcolm Rose

Dance with Death
Jean Ure

13 Murder Mysteries
Various